Silent Mine

A Western Novella

C.M. Saunders

Undertaker Books

For restless spirits everywhere.

SILENT MINE

Santa Ynez Mountains, Western California, 1879

As Dylan Decker entered the saloon and wove his way toward the bar, he habitually allowed his right hand to hover near the leather holster on his hip. He was mindful not to let his hand actually make contact with the handle of the Colt Peacemaker nestled inside. That would send the wrong signal. You wanted people to think you had a gun and knew how to use it, not that you had a gun and couldn't wait to use it.

His boots scuffed the sawdust on the floor, and on looking down he was relieved to find it was still reasonably clean and as yet untainted by spilled liquor or blood. He did his level best to look unperturbed and unimpressed. Image was important. If you looked like a victim, people treated you like one.

The bartender, a tall, wiry-looking man in his early thirties with an impressive handlebar mustache and a scar running the length of his cheek, was busy polishing glasses. Or at least pretending to be. When Dylan approached, he looked up from his work.

"No tab, no ice."

"No problem," Dylan replied. That welcome was all the chill he needed.

"Okay. So now we understand each other, what'll it be, friend?"

"I'll take a gill of whiskey."

"Want a sour toe?" asked the bartender, pointing to a cloudy jar on the counter.

"What's that?"

"A gill of whiskey with a dead man's toe in it. Got the recipe from a bartender up in Dawson City. The toe sets the whiskey off real good and gives it an extra kick, you could say." The bartender smirked at his own joke.

"Where did the toe come from?" asked Dylan, struggling to contain his emotions as they tread the line between disgust and curiosity. He thought he'd seen everything, but this was new to him.

"Off somebody's foot," the bartender snapped with a deadpan expression, what little good will there had once been in his demeanor quickly melting away.

"Do you keep it in that jar of formaldehyde?"

He shrugged. "Where else would I keep it?"

Dylan thought about trying the sour toe for all of three seconds, then declined the generous offer. "If there's no ice I guess I'll just take a whiskey with a splash and pretend I let the ice melt, if it's all the same to you."

"Splash of what?"

"Water," Dylan replied.

"Just water?"

"Yep. Just water."

"How much of a splash?" the bartender asked, as if nobody had ever asked him for a splash of water before.

"As it comes."

"That'll be ten cents," the bartender said, eyeing Dylan up and down with a look somewhere between skepticism and suspicion. This part of the transaction, when actual money changed hands, had obviously gone awry many times before.

Dylan pulled a scuffed leather purse out of his pocket, opened it, and retrieved the money in such a way as to allow the bartender and nobody else a quick peek inside, where several coins lay snugly cocooned, including a shiny silver dollar. People treated you with more respect when they knew you had money.

As he rooted in his purse, a thick-set woman wearing a lop-sided black wig and too much rouge took a position next to him at the counter and intentionally caught his eye. She smiled, showing off a mouth full of decaying teeth. At least they all seemed to be present, which was more than most people could say.

Dylan winked at her. Useful things, winks. It was an understated acknowledgement that simultaneously conveyed a level of understanding. You never knew where the night might lead. At this point he hoped it wouldn't lead him to the bed of a soiled dove, but it never hurt to keep your options open. Taking the hint, the woman nodded discreetly and moved away in search of something more concrete.

The splash of water turned out to be more of a drop, as was usually the case. No bartender wanted a stranger hanging around the place drinking water, even if it was mixed with whiskey. Still, Dylan considered, it was better than having a dead man's severed appendage in his glass. He drained the whiskey in one large gulp, ordered another, and slid another ten cents across the polished wooden counter. That seemed to appease the bartender a little.

Saloons were a refuge. From the elements, from your troubles, from life. Being the focal point, the center of the community where tongues were easily loosened, they were also places strangers went for information. Whether you were looking for some duck eggs or some company, you'd be likely to find it in the saloon.

But there was a downside. There was always a downside.

Saloons in tiny, nondescript frontier towns like Hope's Creek invariably had bad reputations and your first instinct was always to avoid them. They were dangerous, seedy dives populated by drunks, philanderers, gamblers, assorted vagabonds, and people looking for trouble in all its guises. At three in the afternoon, most saloons were perfectly civilized places. It wasn't until around midnight that someone flicked a switch somewhere and everyone lost their minds. That was when the fighting started.

Dylan hoped to be long gone by then.

One thing that didn't change no matter what time of day you visited was the smell. If anything, the merciless afternoon heat only enhanced the stench of whiskey, cigar smoke, stale sweat, old vomit and sawdust. In the far corner, a table of men were playing cards. They looked as if they'd been up for days. Dylan vowed to give them a wide berth. People didn't like being interrupted when they were gambling. Elsewhere, he spied a bald man with wire-framed glasses tottering on a bar stool.

"Passing through?" the bartender asked as he poured the second glass of whiskey. "Hope's Creek ain't the kinda place a man comes unless he has to."

"Right, passing through. Just stopped by your wonderful establishment for a freshen up."

"Are you making a joke about my business?" the bartender said, putting down the whiskey bottle and placing both hands either side of it on the bar. "This establishment, as you call it, is many things but ain't nobody called it 'wonderful' before."

"Not making a joke at all, sir," Dylan replied. "Spending three days and nights out in the open, ridin' from dawn 'til dusk, sleeping on the desert floor, and drinking old pond water when you get thirsty, will make almost anything seem wonderful."

"Ah, I get that. So where ya headed?"

"Looking for a man by the name of Thomas Winstanley. He was last seen around here three or four months ago. Does the name ring a bell?"

"Nope," the bartender shrugged. "To tell the truth, names don't mean much in a place like this."

"Is that right?"

"It sure is. I never even asked yours."

"True. Well, if it'll ease things along, my name's Dylan Decker."

"Doesn't ease things along one bit," the bartender replied. "Your name could be Rutherford B. Hayes and it wouldn't make one bit of difference. I can't tell you what I don't know, and I don't know nothin' about that fella. Why you after him, anyway? You a bounty hunter?"

"Not quite. The man's wife hired me to find him. Last she heard he was out this way prospecting for gold. Stayed here a few weeks and found some old abandoned mine. Then he stopped sending money. Stopped comminicatin', too. She has a kid. The kid needs to eat."

"Don't we all. This old abandoned mine of yours, does it have a name?"

"She said the locals call it Silent Mine."

The bartender suddenly became agitated, and strangely reluctant to look Dylan in the eye. "Never heard of it," he said, picking up a dirty rag and polishing a spot on the bar that was already clean.

"Look," Dylan said, lowering his tone. "This lady needs her husband and the kid needs a daddy. If you don't tell me what I want to know, I'll keep asking 'round until someone else does. I'd wager it won't take very long. Now if I ordered another whiskey and paid triple for it, would you be so kind as to share what you know about this mine?"

"Would you be so kind as to leave right after?" the bartender asked, his discomfort apparent.

"I can see that happening," Dylan nodded. He had just about had his fill of the place anyway.

"Then you got a deal."

"Glad to hear it. One for the road, my good sir."

The bartender took slightly longer than usual to fill Dylan's glass, as if he were still thinking things over. This time, he didn't bother with the splash of water.

Dylan waited patiently. It wasn't the whiskey he wanted, it was information. With the glass in front of him he counted out thirty cents, slid it over the bar, and saw the coins disappear into the bartender's front pocket rather than the cash register.

Formalities concluded and with no other customers at the counter, the bartender leaned in so close to Dylan that his carefully curated whiskers almost brushed his face. Dylan could smell the sourness of his breath.

"Now, I'm telling you this as a friend, friend. Forget whatever this woman told you. Forget about her fella. Forget about Hope's Creek and Silent Mine, and go back to where you came from. You'll find nothing good here, apart from the whiskey."

"Appreciate the concern," Dylan replied, unperturbed, "but that sure as hell ain't gonna happen. I gave that woman my word and I took her hard-earned money. I came this far, and I'm gonna find this Winstanley fella dead or alive, with or without your help. Now tell me everything you know or give me my damn money back."

When all else failed, sometimes the direct approach was best.

The bartender sighed. "Okay, okay. Have it your way. Truth is, I ain't never heard of this fella you're after. But back in the day, Silent Mine brought people from all over. Word had it there were gold nuggets there as big as your fist. I guess some folk still hear the echo, and that's what brought your friend here. If he came at all."

"Back in the day? You mean people don't go up there anymore? It's mined out?"

"Dunno about being mined out, but it's right enough not many folk come looking for it these days. It's more to do with its reputation. Some things are worth more than gold. Let's just say that if this fella disappeared up there, he wouldn't be the first. Just this past year or so, I've heard about five, six, seven, men going missin' up there and there were probably more I didn't hear about. They keep headin' up, and they keep not comin' back. What's a guy like me to do?"

"What happened to them?" Dylan asked pensively.

"If anyone knew that, they wouldn't be missing, would they?"

"S'pose not."

"There's lots of wild animals up there. Mostly wolves and coyotes. Some rattlesnakes. They might account for the odd disappearance or two. There are more than a few bandits roaming the hills, and there are still some Indians left in these parts, too. Mostly Chumash and Miwok. Maybe a few Tolowa or Serrano. They get a bit testy sometimes but mostly keep themselves to themselves. They're afraid to murder too many white folk because of the repercussions. Nah, like I say people go up to that mine to see what's what, and they just don't return. About three years back, a whole family went up there. Stopped in here on the way through, just like you did."

"And?"

"And we never saw 'em again."

"Couldn't they have just struck it rich and moved on someplace else?"

"Not likely. I remember that family well. There were six of them, including two very opinionated brothers about twenty years a'age. If they'd made it big, you can bet the first thing they would've done is come back here shouting their mouths off about it."

"Don't you think all this could be down to rumors? Hearsay?"

"That family was no rumor, friend. I told you, I met 'em myself. Besides, rumors or not, people from away still go there. But the locals, they know better. They know to stay away. Men like you come through looking for people too often for it all to be nothin' but rumors. There's something not right up there at that mine. It's not just dangerous the way other mines are, it's...evil."

"You can't be serious about that."

"I'm deadly serious."

"How do I know you're not on the payroll of some local bigwig hellbent on keeping people away from the place until he mines out all the gold for himself?"

"Frankly, I don't care what you think," the bartender said with a dismissive shrug of his wiry shoulders. "I'm giving you my honest opinion, just like you asked. Believe me, I'd much rather have that mine bursting at the seams. Mining and prospecting is thirsty work. This place would be rammed full every damn night and I might be able to retire early."

Dylan believed him. Like he'd pointed out himself, the bartender had no reason to lie. "I have just one more question, then I'll be out of your hair."

"Shoot."

"Where can I find this unholy place?"

Hope's Creek wasn't quite a one-horse town, but it was close.

And there was very little to be hopeful about.

As he rode Skydance, his trusty five-year-old American Quarter, up Main Street toward the mist-topped mountain range in the distance, Dylan passed a sheriff's office, a barber shop, a butcher, and a bank, interspersed amongst several even more nondescript establishments. On one side of the street, behind the row of shop fronts, was what looked like a boarding house and a small cluster of one-story houses, most of which looked empty.

With only a small number of permanent residents and very little in the way of passing trade, it was clear all the remaining businesses here depended on one another to survive. Since the boom ended, they had all been suffering, and most of the buildings had fallen into a state of disrepair. The windows of some of the older-looking premises had been boarded up, and the spaces between the dilapidated structures were filled with old wagon wheels, carts, and mounds of trash.

Dylan stopped outside the combined general store and post office, dismounted, and tied Skydance to the hitching post. Feeling a little light-headed from the whiskey, he adjusted his gun belt out of habit and entered the building. As he did, a bell attached to the door chimed. The proprietor, an old man with a shock of white hair who'd been hunched over a newspaper looked up, startled.

"Albert Wirrington, at your service!" he announced brightly. "You'll find everything you need and more right here in my amazing general store!"

"Thank you, sir," Dylan replied, wondering how many times Wirrington had dropped that line over the years. "I'm sure we'll be able to do some business."

However, when he let his eyes roam the sparse shelves, Dylan came to doubt the old man's bold assertion. If you wanted dried beans, tinned peaches, or rusted iron nails, you were in luck. But if you were after anything more exotic, you might struggle to find it in Albert Wirrington's amazing general store.

Picking up some dried beans to bulk out his provisions, Dylan took them to the counter. He was heading up into the mountains, and while he liked to think there would be a bountiful supply of food up there, you could never be sure. There was nothing worse than going to sleep on an empty stomach, so it was better to carry some essentials with you. Just in case.

Next to the counter was a basket of almost-fresh carrots, still streaked with soil. Dylan picked out four. One for him and the others as a treat for Skydance.

"Will you be needin' anything else, sir?" Wirrington asked as he rang up the purchases on the cash register. "I have some other things for sale, you know. Things I don't put out on display."

"What things would that be?" asked Dylan, curious.

"Got some worms in today," Wirrington said with a conspiratorial wink.

"Worms, huh?"

"Yep. Worms. Live ones. Wrigglers, too. Thick n' juicy." The old man smacked his lips, as if in the habit of eating worms himself.

"Why do you think I might be needing worms?"

"Fishin'. Why else?"

"I think I'm good for worms," Dylan replied. "Thanks all the same."

"Suit yourself."

"Maybe there is something else you can help me out with," Dylan began. "I'm heading out to Silent Mine. Anything you can tell me about the place?"

Wirrington regarded Dylan with a look somewhere between exasperation and pity. "You sure a fella like you wants to be doing a thing like that? There's better places than that to seek your fortune, ya know."

"That may be. But I'm not going there to seek my fortune. I'm looking for a man named Thomas Winstanley. Last seen in or around that mine. Do you know him?"

"Can't say I do," Wirrington replied, without so much as thinking about it. He suddenly seemed anxious to be rid of Dylan. "And I know most folk around here."

"Never heard the name?"

"'Til just now? Nope. That be all?"

There was something Wirrington wasn't telling him. Dylan could read people well enough to know it. But what could he do? You can't force people to tell you things they don't want to tell you. At least not in a general store in the middle of the afternoon.

"That'll be all," Dylan said as he turned, walked down the aisle and out of the door, making the bell ring again. This time it sounded more like it was mocking rather than welcoming him.

Just before the door swung closed again Wirrington called after him, "You be careful up there!"

Dylan waved a hand in response. He was beginning to get a bad feeling about this Silent Mine.

At the end of Main Street, which should really have been called Only Street, the unpaved road petered out and turned into a dirt track carved out of the earth. As Dylan and Skydance left Hope's Creek behind them, the track became progressively narrower and less defined until it was little more than a pebble-strewn cattle path partly obscured by overhanging bushes and dense vegetation encroaching from both sides.

Dylan looked up at the cloud-studded blue sky and the mountains ahead. There was no sign of civilization, not that he'd been expecting any. The bartender at the saloon had told him to expect nothing apart from the odd hunting lodge and a few old cabins up around the mine. Not that it bothered him. He felt at home in the wild, and on the move. He was used to it. Where people went, trouble usually followed.

His parents had come to America shortly before Dylan was born, transplanting themselves from the coalfields of the south Wales valleys to the coalfields of Pennsylvania, where their skills were in demand and the pay was better. It was a new start for them, and all they must have seen were limitless possibilities. Before long they were able to buy their own plot of land, the dream being to eventually work for themselves rather than line the pockets of others, and settled into the community. They must have felt so proud, and so free.

But it was a hard life for them. As a boy, Dylan remembered seeing the network of blue scars criss-crossing his father's frail body as he lay in bed wheezing and coughing up black phlegm, his damaged lungs stuttering and fighting for each breath. He died before he was fifty. That was the way with career miners. The end game. Some would say it was the best they could hope for, and perhaps the only way to avoid such a demise would be a premature death underground.

Neither option appealed much to Dylan, so the day he turned twenty he left the family home to blaze his own trail. That had been almost twelve years ago. He felt guilty about leaving his mother, but she was a strong woman and didn't want to hold him back.

Besides, his sister Rebecca, who'd arrived three years after him, was a homebody and had no intention of going anywhere. She had a child of her own now, having married a traveling salesman. When he was around, he stayed with them, otherwise it was just mom, Rebecca, and baby Dawn, three generations living under the same roof. And they wouldn't have it any other way.

He had yet to settle and start his own family, so Dylan visited them in Pennsylvania every so often, staying for a couple of weeks to rest up, until that world began to feel too small and he'd be off on his travels again.

When he was away he wired some money to the family every few months just to make sure the girls didn't go without. He knew George did the same, and Rebecca made her own money sewing. Between that and the pension from the mine his father had worked, they had more than enough for their needs.

Dylan lived a simple life. He went from place to place doing various odd jobs, from fruit picking to bounty hunting. He enjoyed the sense of freedom, of being in control of his own destiny. He'd just come to the end of a two-month stint as a farmhand in Iowa when his boss asked if he minded having a look for Thomas Winstanley on behalf of a friend of his. A female friend. Dylan didn't ask questions. That was generally how things happened. Word of mouth. Recommendations. Turns out, there were a lot of people in the world who needed things done.

He'd been reluctant at first. It sounded like an impossible task. Mrs. Winstanley didn't give him much to go on, but she had given him fifty dollars, plus the promise of another fifty should he find her husband or some proof of what had happened to him, which was more than enough to maintain Dylan's interest. At least for a while.

He swapped a few telegrams with her, and she seemed like a nice lady. A nice lady who wanted answers. With nothing else lined up, Dylan even considered doing the job for free. He was sensitive to her plight, and got the impression they were cut from the same cloth. Miners were miners, and had a code of honor as binding as anyone else's. The only difference between them was that her family had been chasing the kind of gold that sparkled in the sun, while his family had been more invested in the black kind you burned in your hearth.

If you were going to spend as much time traveling alone through the predator-filled wilderness and lawless hick towns as Dylan, you needed to be able to defend yourself. Apart from his cherished .45 caliber Colt Peacemaker, boasting an intricately engraved barrel and his initials carved into the ivory grip, Dylan's main weapon was a .44 Winchester rifle with twenty-inch barrel he carried in a long holster fastened to Skydance's saddle bag. Equally useful with regards to hunting as self-defense, he didn't know where he would be without his repeater. His model was a classic 1873 he'd bought from a cattle rancher three years earlier. It was probably time he upgraded to one of the newer models, but he just couldn't bring himself to part with it. Breaking in new weapons was every bit as painful and troublesome as breaking in new boots, and could be a lot more hazardous to your health.

His third gun was a twin-barrelled Model 95 Remington Derringer, known as a Double Derringer, that he kept hidden in a specially fashioned pouch in his right boot. It was his last resort, and he was grateful that so far he hadn't been pressed into using it. Due to the small caliber slug, slow reload time, and effective range of just a few feet, it was next to useless in a fire fight. He kept it more for peace of mind than anything else, knowing that if he was ever disarmed he would have something to defend himself with apart from his fists.

Elsewhere on his person, Dylan routinely carried about a dozen spare cartridges for the Colt and a Bowie knife in a sheath on his belt. The rest of his worldly belongings, what little there were, were stowed in the saddlebags: woolen blankets, camping and cooking utensils, matches, a poncho, some spare clothes, canteens, a box of rifle ammo, rope, and a copy of his favorite book, Jules Verne's *Twenty Thousand Leagues Under the Sea*. He'd read it five or six times already, and intended to trade it in next time he visited his mother's house, where the family kept a collection of his father's books.

The tattered, water-damaged, dog-eared book was his only luxury, and he hadn't been without one science fiction novel or another since being introduced to the genre by his dad as a kid. He was completely seduced by the promise of dropping in and out of the kind of fantastical worlds that existed so far beyond anything he could imagine. Dylan's father had done a lot for him, but giving him an appreciation of the written word was perhaps the greatest single thing.

He traveled as lightly as he could because unlike most people, he didn't attach much value to material possessions. His priorities may change in the future, but right now the experience of living well was the best reward he could hope for and accumulating wealth was an empty pursuit. It just meant there was more to carry.

Plus, Skydance wouldn't be overjoyed about it.

He was a good horse, fast and strong, and lugging around a pile of crap would only slow him down. Still, Dylan would be lying if he said he hadn't fantasized about finding a hoard of gold at Silent Mine.

According to the bartender, the mine was a day's ride from Hope's Creek, but shouldn't be too difficult to find. He just had to follow the path up into the mountains, bear right into the gorge, then pass a small freshwater lake, and the mine would be right there. The directions sounded vague, but in Dylan's experience, anything man-made in an otherwise untouched landscape stood out for miles. Plus, he hadn't discounted stumbling across a sign post at some point.

On the path ahead two unmistakable shapes began to emerge from the leafy terrain, bringing Dylan's senses swiftly back into focus.

Men on horseback.

The sight instantly put Dylan on edge. Most people you met out in the countryside were civil. Friendly, even. There was an element of camaraderie binding those cast adrift, and a sense that everyone's lives would be easier if only they could all pull in the same direction. Most recognized that they were all in the same position, fighting the same common enemies in the form of hostile locals, the elements, the wildlife, and even the land itself, which fought back with more ferocity than any human or animal ever could, and any misfortune that befell a comrade could just as easily happen to you.

Still, there were a few bad eggs who wanted whatever you had, even if what you had didn't amount to much. They weren't to know that until they saw it for themselves. For all any stranger knew, Dylan's saddle bags might be loaded full of gold or silver. Being alone with nobody to rely on, he had to mind himself. Suspicion was a loner's best friend.

As the figures drew closer, Dylan saw there were two men riding side by side on tired, old horses. Probably some kind of hunting party. One was dressed in a brown hide coat and wore a large sombrero-type hat that obscured most of his face, while the other was a younger, confident-looking man in shirtsleeves. His blonde hair was being ruffled by the wind, and there was a double-barrelled shotgun across his lap.

When they saw Dylan, the two men exchanged a few words, then slipped into single file with Sombrero Guy taking the lead. Dylan might have been overreacting, but something about the men, and the situation, was making him nervous.

He carefully edged Skydance onto the extreme left of the path to give the men room to pass and held the reins steady with one hand while resting the other on his Colt, just so the strangers would know it was there.

"Howdy, friend," Sombrero Guy said, raising a hand to his brow in a faux salute.

"Howdy yourselves," Dylan replied with as much enthusiasm as he could muster.

The younger guy with the shotgun said nothing, instead offering a toothy smile that made him look like he wasn't playing with a full deck.

As they passed close enough to touch, Dylan studied the pair out of the corner of his eye. Neither of the strangers seemed to pose much of an immediate threat, but the younger man looked a little trigger happy and rambunctious. The younger ones generally were. They tended to slow down later in life, if they made it that far.

Without warning, Smiler dug his spurs into his horse's hindquarters and jerked the reins at the same time, making the dirty white mare rear up.

Skydance let out a startled snort and instinctively recoiled. It was all Dylan could do to restrain him. Everything was happening so fast, and Dylan smelt a rat. Sombrero Guy was now behind him, blocking any retreat. Dylan drew his Colt and spun around to see if Sombrero Guy had drawn his.

He hadn't. He simply hung back, watching events unfold with a cold glint in his eye. When he saw Dylan's Colt, he calmly showed him both palms.

Smiler had now managed to sheath his shotgun and was gradually bringing his horse under control, "There now, there now," he cooed. "Sorry 'bout that," he said to Dylan, showing that smile again. "She's a lil' skittish is all. Could do with getting some discipline. Like most females."

"No problem," Dylan said, feeling like a prized fool as he slipped his Colt back into its holster. "These things happen."

"If you don't mind me saying, you're mighty keen to pull that gun," Sombrero Guy said, his tone low and measured.

"Can't be too careful," Dylan replied, wondering if he'd put his Colt away too soon.

"Hear that, hear that. So what brings you up this way?"

"Lookin' for a friend," Dylan said. He considered asking the men if they'd heard of Thomas Winstanley, but thought better of it. If neither the bartender nor shopkeeper at the nearest town knew of the man, he doubted these two would. Besides, the less they knew about him and his business, the better.

"Well, I sure hope you find him," Sombrero Guy said, tugging on his horse's reins and continuing on his way.

As the younger blonde guy passed, he flashed another of his trademark grins. Only now, Dylan could see there was no trace of warmth in it.

-III-

The incident with the pair of strangers might have amounted to nothing, but as he and Skydance trudged on through the fading autumn light higher and higher into the mountains, Dylan found he was unable to put it out of his mind. The young blonde guy with the fake smile had made his mare rear up on him deliberately. Dylan was sure of it. But why?

Just for the hell of it?

To try to give Dylan a fright?

No, his actions had been calculated, carefully executed, and didn't contain even the smallest element of frivolity.

To prove a point, then. That was more like it. But if that were the case, Dylan was missing the point the pair had put so much effort into making. It was a puzzling state of affairs, but one thing he'd come to learn was that nobody did anything for nothing. There was a motive behind everything, however much people tried to hide it.

A chilly wind was beginning to blow and it would soon be too dark to navigate unfamiliar territory. He'd been pushing Skydance most of the day, and the horse could do with a rest.

Dylan reached into the nearest saddle bag, rummaged around, and retrieved one of the carrots he'd purchased at the general store in Hope's Creek.

"Not much further, boy," he said, holding the carrot for the horse to eat and rubbing a spot behind his ear as he snaffled it down.

The path had led them into a gorge where it merged with a natural trail meandering through the increasingly difficult terrain. On either side mountains rose up like giant tombstones studded with sparse patches of spiky vegetation, and overhead a solitary vulture circled.

Suddenly, the crack of a gunshot shattered the stillness. Dylan instinctively drew his Colt for the second time that day and spun around, trying to look in every direction at once.

Nothing stirred. Even the wildlife, probably as spooked by the shot as he was, had fallen silent.

A quick check revealed that neither he nor Skydance was hit and he hadn't heard any ricochet, which suggested the gunfire hadn't been directed at them. Why would it be? Gunshots were far from uncommon. More than likely, someone nearby was hunting dinner and the fact that there were no follow-on shots seemed to confirm it. What nobody wanted to hear out in the wilderness was a flurry of gunfire, which would indicate there were either two parties going at it, or you were coming under attack.

Satisfied he and Skydance were in no immediate danger, Dylan put away his revolver once more and pressed on with even more care. Now his priorities had changed. When he'd left Hope's Creek he'd harbored vague aspirations of locating Silent Mine before nightfall, but that was becoming more unlikely by the minute. He decided he might be better off finding somewhere to camp for the night and continuing the trek in the morning.

Not long after, the freshwater lake came into view, just as the bartender had said it would. It was indeed small. So small that it was more of a pond than a lake. What was the difference between a large pond and a small lake? This one probably doubled or tripled in size when the rain and melted snow ran down off the mountain. The closer Dylan got, the more tranquil and inviting the lake looked as the last vestiges of sunlight reflected off the gently rippling surface.

Suddenly, a flash of movement at the water's far edge caught his eye, and he gently brought Skydance to a stop. There, partially obscured by a clump of bushes, was a deer drinking. Judging by the size, it was little more than a fawn. Dylan glanced down at the stock of his Winchester. The deer hadn't seen or smelled him yet. The breeze was in his favor. But it could change at any moment. If he acted now, he'd be able to aim and get a shot off. Maybe even two or three, depending on which direction the animal ran, which should be more than enough to bring it down before it found cover.

But he couldn't do it. As hungry as he was, he was too awestruck by the deer's grace and beauty to slaughter it just to fill a hole in his stomach. A fish or a hare would fill that hole just the same, and there would be no waste. There was a lot of meat on that deer. Probably enough to last him a week or more. But he had no means of preserving it, and in these moderate temperatures it would start to rot inside a day. Within two, it would be riddled with fly eggs and maggots. Plus, firing his gun would not only spoil the calmness and scare off every animal within a two-mile radius, but also draw attention. That was something only a fool did. When you were on your own, it usually paid to keep a low profile.

Dylan decided the bank of the lake would make an ideal place to camp, and after hitching Skydance to a sturdy tree overlooking the water, close enough that he could drink his fill without too much trouble, he relieved the horse of his saddlebags, fed him the rest of his carrots, then turned his attention to his own dinner. Being the only source of drinking water for some distance, the lake would naturally attract animals so all he would have to do was find a spot down wind and be ready.

But of course that was a double-edged sword. For every plump rabbit or elk that wandered over, there would be a coyote or a wolf. There were also bears in the area, grizzlies, who would be looking to fatten themselves up before hibernating for the winter.

You could never really relax when you were sleeping out in the open. Dylan treated himself to a bunkhouse or even a hotel room a couple of nights a month, depending on where in the world he found himself, and providing they weren't too expensive. All he really needed was a bed and a bath. The biggest advantage, and the thing he appreciated most, was having a lock on the door. It's the simple things.

There were no locked doors out in the open.

Sometimes he wondered if part of the attraction was the slow-burning tension and underlying sense of vulnerability that came with this existence. The danger, and the constant feeling that anything could happen at any time. It heightened his senses and made him feel alive. Sure, a nice little job with a settled life somewhere would have its advantages, but would it truly satisfy him? He didn't think so. All that mundane drudgery, living to pay bills, and doing the same things every day not because you wanted to, but because you had to, would be soul destroying to a free spirit like him.

The edges of the lake were littered with a variety of tracks, both old and new, and several little paths where the sparse vegetation had been almost completely cleared veered off in different directions. Dylan was happy to see that all the tracks belonged to animals, and there were no signs of any people apart from what appeared to be the remnants of a long-abandoned campsite on the opposite side of the lake.

He'd given up on the idea of shooting his supper, and decided instead to try his hand at fishing instead. The water was crystal clear, and with so few people and predators around, the lake would be teeming with fish. Probably bass or trout, he reckoned. He always carried fishing gear in his saddlebags, some lengths of line and a few different sized hooks, and over the years had polished his skills to a reasonably high level. Or so he liked to think. But fishing was one of those pursuits you never really mastered. There was always room for improvement.

Settling on a spot a little upwind from where he had tethered Skydance, Dylan quickly cleared the area of any sharp rocks to make it a little more comfortable. Then he collected some fire wood and a few handfuls of dried grass and twigs for kindling, dug a shallow pit, and got a fire going. When sleeping out in the open, a fire was crucial so he always made it a priority. Daylight hours were cool, even in early winter, but the nights could get bitterly cold in the mountains and a blanket just wasn't enough. A fire not only provided heat and light, but kept any wild animals at bay. If he felt like a challenge he would go about it the old-fashioned way by rubbing two sticks together, but that could take hours. Tonight, he used his matches.

With the fire lit, he found some bait under a rock, a fat wriggling worm that Albert Wirrington would be proud of, pierced it with one of the hooks, attached a small pebble to the line to give it some weight, and cast it out into the lake. He was prepared for a long wait. It was never easy to catch a fish. They weren't as stupid as people liked to think, and wanted to survive as much as the next creature.

But the worm proved irresistible, and Dylan was getting nibbles almost immediately. The moment it felt like something worth the trouble was taking the bait, he yanked the line to sink the hook in the fish's mouth and began hauling it in hand over hand.

He could tell by the weight and how much it struggled that his catch was a decent size, and he wasn't disappointed. It was a brown trout, at least fifteen or sixteen inches long, meaning it would provide at least a pound of succulent white meat. Enough for a decent supper and maybe even a bit of breakfast. That was about as good as life got.

He wasted no time gutting and boning the fish with his Bowie knife, throwing the stringy handful of guts back in the water like a peace offering. They were no use to him, and if he left them rotting on the bank God only knew what they might attract. Finally, he sharpened a stick he found on the bank of the lake, skewered the fish through the side, and roasted it over the fire.

He hungrily ate the trout as the day eventually surrendered to the night, slurping at the bones before throwing them in the fire. When he finished, he spent a few minutes cleaning his knife and sharpening it with a stone. It was therapeutic. Finally, he threw a couple of chunky logs on the fire to keep it burning into the night, wrapped a blanket around himself, and fell asleep listening to the soothing rhythm of the water lapping against the shore.

-IV-

Dylan's eyes snapped open.

There were noises disrupting the stillness of the night, pulling him back from the warm embrace of sleep.

It sounded like something was circling his camp, scuffing the soil and snapping twigs underfoot. He opened half an eye. The fire had been reduced to nothing but glowing embers, and above was a sprawling landscape of twinkling stars with the moon as a centerpiece like a jewel in a crown, its effervescent light reflecting off the gently rippling surface of the lake.

Despite his heart now thudding somewhere near his throat, Dylan lay as still as he could. Whatever was here with him hadn't attacked yet, and him suddenly leaping into life could be perceived as threatening behavior. Such a move could spur the prowler into either striking or taking flight, and it was impossible to know which way things would go. The last thing he wanted was to get injured this far from civilization. He would bleed out or die of exposure long before he could make it back to Hope's Creek.

It's probably just a curious coyote, he told himself, not very convincingly.

By now, whatever it was had edged its way over to Skydance and Dylan's saddlebags, which were just outside his field of vision. From his prone position he strained his ears, and heard the buckle on one of them being gently unfastened. That could only mean one thing. His nocturnal visitor was no animal. He was being robbed.

Giving up on playing possum, Dylan quickly rose to a sitting position, threw off the blanket, drew his Colt and cocked it. This was one of those occasions where it paid to sleep wearing a gun belt.

His suspicions were correct. Because his eyes were still adjusting to the gloom he couldn't make out any details, but found himself staring directly at the figure of a man mostly obscured by shadows with his arm elbow-deep in one of Dylan's saddlebags.

"Stop what you're doing," Dylan said, his deep voice breaking the thick silence.

The figure froze, and Skydance gave a disgusted little snort accompanied by a shake of the head as if to scold Dylan's belated intervention.

It's about time you showed up.

A dozen scenarios played out in Dylan's mind simultaneously. He still wasn't quite sure what was going on, let alone what he should do next. It was clear he was being robbed, but the 'who' and 'why' escaped him and he was reluctant to pull the trigger until he had more of a handle on the situation. When you started shooting there was no putting the genie back in the bottle or the bullets back in the gun.

What happened next changed everything.

"I suggest you put down that piece, friend. Unless you wanna be wearing your insides as a fashion accessory."

The voice came from behind him. There was someone else. And that low, droning voice was familiar. Cursing his stupidity at allowing himself to be blind-sided so easily, Dylan slowly turned around.

Just the stranger's silhouette was enough to tell Dylan who he was.

Sombrero Guy, and this time it was him brandishing the double-barrelled shotgun.

Dylan hadn't let his Colt waiver from its original target, who no doubt was the blonde-haired guy with the fake smile, and he quickly ran through his options. He could drop Smiler easily enough, but by the time he turned his gun on Sombrero Guy he'd be full of buckshot. Every nerve in his body told him to do it, take the chance. The shotgun might not even be loaded, and even if it was, Sombrero Guy might not have the gall to use it.

But if it was loaded and he did have the gall to use it, it would be all over.

Dylan fought back the rising tide of emotion and struggled to retain control. He was alone out here, and outnumbered by at least two to one. He had to stay calm and try to find a way out of this situation.

The men had followed him, and waited until he was asleep to strike. Cowards.

As the realization set in, Dylan knew ultimately, they were going to kill him. Guys like them didn't leave victims standing. Survivors meant witnesses, and witnesses meant trouble. Lawbreakers didn't want their nefarious activities to be reported to the local authorities, and they certainly didn't want anyone going after them with revenge in mind because that would mean constantly looking over their shoulders. Who knew how many people they'd robbed, murdered, and left out here to rot?

"What do you want from me?" Dylan asked, just about managing to keep his voice on an even keel.

"We ain't fussy," Sombrero Guy said. "We had a good look-see at you earlier, and we know you don't got much. We'd get something for your horse and that Colt is worth a few dollars by the looks, the repeater over there a few more. No doubt you got a stash o' cash hidden somewhere, fellas like you normally do, but I doubt it'll be a very big stash. Still, you never know. We might get lucky. See, we kinda get the impression you're out here prospecting. You might've had a good day yesterday and have a saddlebag full of gold."

"That'd be wishful thinking on your part. If I had a saddlebag full of gold, don't you think I'd be back in town raving it up in the saloon?"

Skydance gave another timely little snort as if in agreement.

"Well," Sombrero Guy said, "I ain't got no answer to that. I don't know you. Maybe you just ain't very smart. What's in them bags, Billy?"

"Nothin' yet."

Dylan could hear the younger man rooting through his possessions, and it made him seethe with anger. His finger began to caress the trigger of his revolver and he had to physically force himself to relax.

He needed to think up a plan.

Fast.

"Now do as I say, friend, and toss that piece you're holding my way before we have some kinda misunderstanding," Sombrero Guy drawled. "Misunderstandings out here can be dangerous."

Feeling an almost physical wrench as the gun left his hand, Dylan did as the man asked. He needed to stall for time, and couldn't help feeling that if he didn't follow instructions Sombrero Guy was going to shoot. Him being alive or dead made no difference to these crooks. In fact, he'd be a lot less trouble dead.

"Why haven't you killed me already?" he asked, genuinely curious.

"Because dead men can't talk," Sombrero Guy replied ominously. "It'll be easier all 'round if you tell us what ya got and where it is. But whether you tell us or not, we'll find it anyway. If we don't find anything, we've lost nothing. If we find somethin' good, well, it'd be like Christmas morning for me and young William over there. And we do like Christmas mornin', don't we William?"

"That we do!"

"Since you're obviously not content to just raid my possessions," Dylan said, eager to move things along to their inevitable conclusion, "what exactly is it that you fellas want me to talk about?"

"You look like a man who knows his stuff, and we want to know where you're going. You wouldn't be out here without some good information. We're figuring we can follow the bird to the nest, if ya catch my drift."

"And pick on some other innocent folk?"

"Innocent?" Sombrero Guy cackled. "I don't know what rock you been livin' under, but ain't nobody innocent these days. So c'mon, friend. Where's the gold?"

"I don't know any more than you. I just got here, remember?"

"So tell us where you're headed."

"I'm on my way to that place they call Silent Mine," Dylan replied, an idea finally forming in his head. "Heard good things about the place."

The twin shotgun barrels pointing at him suddenly twitched. Dylan braced himself for the boom, or the flash, but none came and he breathed a sigh of relief.

For a few seconds, Sombrero Guy said nothing. Finally, he drawled, "Won't find much up there, friend. Damn place is cursed."

Now, Dylan's curiosity was seriously piqued. "What makes you say that?"

"Didn't ya know? People go in there, and they don't come back out."

"Like who?"

"Like my brother-in-law, Joe. Oh, seven or eight summers ago now. He was an honest, working man. Went up to Silent Mine to do some digging, and that was the last anyone ever saw of him."

"If your sister is anything like you, he probably did a runner."

There was a pause, then Sombrero Guy laughed. "Maybe he did. I can't say I'd blame him one bit. Do you know what the Chumash say about it?"

"Nope."

"They say there's a crack in the earth up there, in or around the mine, and that crack is the gateway to another world or somethin'. They couldn't believe us whitey would be so stupid as to go in there of our own accord."

"Why so?"

"Because that other world is filled with monsters, the kind that'll put your worst nightmare to shame, and them monsters find you accordin' to the noises you make. That's where the name Silent Mine comes from. You gotta be quiet. You make any noise, and them monsters come and rip you apart. Have you ever tried being quiet in a mine?"

"Can't say I have." Dylan was being honest. He had never even set foot inside a mine.

"Well, it ain't easy," Sombrero Guy said. "There's the sounds of tools, digging, people talking. Maybe the odd explosion. Them sounds carry for miles underground."

"So you think the monsters got them?"

"Would explain a lot, don'tcha think?"

"Hey!" the young blonde guy suddenly yelled, interrupting the conversation. "I think I found something!"

"What is it?" Sombrero Guy said, practically bouncing on his haunches with excitement.

"Hid in the bottom of the bag. Feels big n' hard!"

In his eagerness to inspect their haul Sombrero Guy was now on his tiptoes, craning his neck in the direction of his companion.

"Wait," the younger guy said, his smile faltering as he waved something in the air above his head. "What the heck is this?"

"It's a book," Dylan said.

"I can see that!" Sombrero Guy said with disdain.

"Then why ask what it is?"

"I mean... I mean what kind of book is it?" Sombrero Guy replied.

"It's *Twenty Thousand Leagues Under the Sea.* Can't you read?" Dylan said. He was losing patience. The very thought of these low-lifes fingering his most prized possessions made his skin crawl.

"No," Sombrero Guy retorted without a trace of irony. "Never learned. Why do you have it?"

"Fine, fine," Dylan said, trying his best to inject some passable crushing disappointment into his tone. His plan was beginning to come to fruition. "You caught me out. I'll come clean, if you let me go, okay?"

"Sure, sure. We'll let you go," Smiler said a little too enthusiastically. Dylan saw he and Sombrero Guy exchange a quick glance that was as good as a death sentence.

"You can find the answers you seek in the book."

Both assailants paused to consider Dylan's words.

"Must be a hiding place!" Sombrero Guy shouted at his companion. "Maybe he hollowed out the middle and put his valuables in there. Prolly wasn't countin' on meeting anyone as smart as us. Hurry up and check it!"

The twin barrels of the shotgun had now wavered so much they weren't even pointing at Dylan anymore. He saw his opportunity, immediately recognizing that it might be his *only* opportunity. Still, if he was going down, he was going down with a roar rather than a whimper.

With Sombrero Guy distracted, Dylan knelt, unholstered his Derringer, and aimed it at his would-be assailant. Knowing the time for talking had passed, he fired both barrels without warning, the double report shattering the stillness of the night and reverberating around the mountains.

The first bullet went wild, but it didn't matter. The second went through Sombrero Guy's right eye, exploding it on impact. The single line of blood running down his cheek was black in the moonlight. His eyebrows arched and his lower jaw sagged open as if he'd been in the act of saying something important as he keeled over dead, the sombrero askew but still affixed.

With Dylan's senses now heightened, everything seemed to be happening in slow motion. He didn't know if Smiler was armed so he ducked his head and rolled out of the way of any return fire, plucking his Colt up off the ground as he came out of it. From a crouching position, he leveled the weapon at the younger man who stood dumbly clutching Dylan's book. There was a look of confusion on his face, as if he couldn't quite comprehend what was happening.

In Dylan's mind, it wasn't so complicated. What did these dimwits think he was going to do? Lie down and let them rob him blind as a precursor to murdering him?

Too late, Smiler realized their plan was going off the rails and dropped the book. It thudded on the ground, sending an irrational jolt of rage through Dylan. How could this parasite treat a book with such contempt? And not just any book. His favorite book.

For the briefest moment, everything was in the balance.

Was Smiler going to run or attack?

He didn't seem quite sure what he was going to do himself, and for a few seconds did a funky little hip dance as he transferred his weight rapidly from one foot to the other and back again. Then, with a defiant yell, the young delinquent took a few lurching steps toward Dylan and swung a boot at his face.

Dylan should have reacted sooner. But he hesitated for a moment, giving Smiler the benefit of the doubt, and he paid a heavy price for it. The boot struck him under the chin, smashing his teeth together with a sickening crunch and sending him reeling backwards.

Lying on his back in the dirt, he didn't know how many of the pinpricks of light dancing in front of his eyes were stars in the sky and how many were a result of the blow.

As his mouth and throat filled up with chipped teeth and the coppery taste of blood, he thought about how easy it would be to just drift away and let it all happen.

One by one, the stars overhead began to blink out. Part of Dylan welcomed the all-consuming darkness. It would be so easy to succumb. All he had to do was nothing.

But a more substantial part of him was still burning with rage at the injustice of it all.

Who did these fools think they were? Coming into his camp, pushing him around, making threats, disrespecting his possessions?

Coming fully to his senses he realized the boot was now hovering above his face preparing to stomp him.

In his mind's eye he saw his skull splitting open, spilling blood and brains into the dirt like foul soup.

Not today.

Throwing up his hands, he caught the boot, held it, and twisted sharply to his side bringing the owner of the boot crashing down.

There was a scramble, and Dylan somehow found himself on the bottom. He was bigger than Smiler, but the smaller man was much stronger than his wiry frame suggested, something that became even more evident when he closed his hands around Dylan's throat and started squeezing.

He was going to choke the life out of him.

Dylan tried throwing punches, but from his prone position couldn't generate enough power to do any real damage and was only able to land glancing blows.

The younger man's face was so close to Dylan's he could smell his rancid breath. He was smiling again. Or maybe it was a grimace. It was difficult to tell in the moonlight.

Dylan cringed and screwed up his face as a disgusting globule of stringy white saliva worked its way out of Smiler's open mouth and dropped into Dylan's lips.

He had to do something to stop the onslaught before he was overpowered. Instead of lashing out, he grabbed at Smiler's face, latching on and digging his fingers into his eye sockets.

The younger man howled with a mixture of rage and pain, let go of Dylan's throat, and scrambled to his feet.

At the same time, Dylan snatched up his Colt.

Right there was Smiler's chance to run away. And if he'd chosen that route, in all likelihood Dylan would have let him go.

But Smiler didn't want that. Filled with the petulance of youth, he instead reached for something out of view, probably a gun or a knife tucked into his belt or waistband.

It occurred to Dylan that as cold and calculating as this man, who was really little more than a boy, appeared, it was possible he might not be playing with a full deck. Dylan wasn't in the business of taking advantage of people, so he decided to give Smiler one final chance to get out alive and shouted, "Don't do it!"

Smiler did it anyway.

To his own detriment, he had moved to the right of Skydance and now stood silhouetted against the shimmering surface of the lake. In one fluid motion, Dylan cocked the revolver and pulled the trigger.

While the Derringer had made a loud *pop*, the larger caliber Colt boomed as it unleashed hell upon the young transgressor. At a range of barely ten feet, the bullet hit him in the chest and propelled him backward. As he staggered, pinwheeling his arms in a bid to regain his balance, Dylan pulled the trigger again. The second bullet also found its target and must have hit a vital organ because it quickly put an end to the struggle. No way was anyone coming back from a pair of .45 slugs in the trunk.

There was a loud splash, and Smiler landed in the water with his arms splayed out either side of him, as if he were making a snow angel.

He wasn't smiling any more.

Dylan didn't feel any guilt or remorse. As far as he was concerned, he had done only what he had to do to survive, and if he hadn't acted it would be him lying dead now while the pair of crooks helped themselves to all his belongings.

But now he had to get out of the area fast.

It was still nighttime, but you never knew who might be in earshot and decide to come investigate the commotion, hoping to pick up the pieces. He was the innocent party here, the one who had been attacked. All he'd done was defend himself. But he had no proof of that and it was his word against two dead men.

Dylan quickly searched Sombrero Guy's body, finding nothing but a half-empty pouch of chewing tobacco, a handful of coins and a few shotgun shells. The shotgun itself had seen better days and wasn't worth much. If he took it, it would only weigh him down. Plus, it would link him to what had happened here. So instead, he threw it into the lake. Then, he kicked dirt over the campfire to make sure it was out, loaded up Skydance, and hit the trail again.

He left Sombrero Guy where he lay. It was what he and Smiler would've done to him. Within days the local wildlife would strip the flesh and scatter the bones far and wide, leaving practically no trace.

The last thing Dylan did before leaving camp was find his assailant's horses, which they'd hitched a few hundred yards away. They were skittish, no surprise there, but seemed grateful when Dylan cut off their saddles and let them loose. Much like their previous owners, they were free now.

-V-

Some might call navigating your way through unfamiliar, hostile terrain in the dark a challenge. Others might call it downright stupid. Skydance could easily turn over on one of his legs, or even break one. That would be bad for the horse, but worse for Dylan. It would leave him a day's ride from the nearest town with no horse and limited supplies.

That was why sensible people traveled during daylight hours and rested at night. To avoid any mishaps, Dylan and Skydance were going to have to take it slow and steady until sunrise.

It hurt when Dylan swallowed and his mouth was still bleeding. He had to spit every few yards to keep his airways clear. Gently probing a large cut on the inside of his upper lip with his tongue, he realized the little shit who'd dropped his book in the dirt had not only chipped a few but knocked one of his front teeth loose.

Wonderful.

Eating would be difficult for a while, and the injury would probably make his whole face swell up like a watermelon.

It made Dylan want to kill him all over again.

The reduced pace together with the poor night's sleep, his injuries, and the adrenaline dump following the gunfight combined to make Dylan drowsy. It was all he could do to keep his eyes open. Alternating between being fully alert and lapsing into a semi-dream state, it was a struggle just to keep his thoughts moving in a straight line, let alone Skydance.

His mind kept drifting away into his past, while he slipped his fingers under his shirt cuff and felt along the long, jagged scar on his forearm. He didn't keep track of the men he killed, just like he didn't keep score of the women he slept with, but he remembered the first. Just like women, you always remembered the first.

It was deep in an Arizona winter and he'd just turned twenty-three. He'd been riding solo for almost three years, and found himself caught up in a turf war between two ranches. Donovan's, where Dylan worked, and a near neighbor. Sometimes, when you were hired as a ranch hand, you were expected to help out in any way that was needed, and that included being the muscle.

One night, the rival ranch sent over a gang to burn down Donovan's barns and cowsheds. With the animals still inside. Unfortunately for them, they were caught red handed.

A fight ensued which soon escalated and left two men dead and three more badly wounded. There was an unspoken agreement between the warring factions not to use guns when they clashed. If they did, there would've been a lot more bloodshed and a lot more attention. Instead, both sides used knives and clubs, knuckledusters and chains.

During the melee a man came at Dylan, a dueling knife in each hand. He was obviously well trained, and operating far above Dylan's level. He knew if he was going to come out of it alive he had to strike first, and strike hard. He pulled his Bowie knife, the same one he still wore fastened to his belt, and charged. More through luck than judgment the blade embedded itself deep in the knifeman's guts, but not before Dylan had taken some damage.

Even at that tender age Dylan had seen people stabbed before, and it was never a clean kill. Never pretty, either. It wasn't like you just jabbed a knife in someone and they obediently dropped to the floor in a dead heap. More than likely, it would just make them mad. He'd seen people get stabbed two, three times, then sit down and finish a card game while they waited for the doctor to come and stitch them up.

Dylan hadn't wanted to go blow for blow with the knife-wielding lunatic, so when the Bowie was buried to the hilt in his adversary's stomach, he dragged it down, twisted it, and then pulled it across.

The sharp steel cut effortlessly through skin and muscle, tipping a deluge of blood and intestines over his hand and wrist, the viscera steaming in the freezing temperatures. As the man dropped, mortally wounded, Dylan noticed for the first time a wedding ring on his finger. That brought home the fragility of life. The man who lay dying at his feet was someone's husband, someone's son, and maybe someone's father. He likely had as much personal interest in this skirmish as Dylan did, and was probably just doing what his boss wanted. It took a long time for Dylan to reconcile the fact that it had been kill or be killed.

When the fight was over and both sides retreated to count their casualties and lick their wounds, his boss, Mr. Donovan, said it would probably be best all around if Dylan moved on that night. He called in the local Doc to patch up a slash on his forearm. Then he thanked Dylan for his service, gave him two weeks' cash-in-hand, let him choose a horse from the stable, and promised to tell anyone who came looking for him that he had done a midnight flit and he had no idea where he was. The plan must have worked, because nobody had caught up with Dylan.

Yet.

But there was always that element of doubt in his mind. Every morning he woke up wondering if this would be the day he was finally called to account and made to pay for his crimes. Even if he managed to evade the clutches of the lawmen and bounty hunters, escaping the retribution of the universe was another matter entirely. Dylan believed good things happened to good people, and vice versa. Nobody could be good all the time; we're all engaged in a kind of life-long balancing act constantly weighing up the things we did and the things we wanted to do.

There were no two ways about it, Dylan had a lot to atone for.

When the first rays of sunlight finally penetrated the inky darkness, the landscape around him changed, along with Dylan's mood. The tiredness was still with him, but beaten into submission by that new-found sense of optimism that accompanies first light.

Having emerged victorious from a difficult night, he felt as if he'd turned a corner. The local wildlife must have shared his good cheer, because soon the air was full of birdsong.

Dylan sucked in a deep breath of fresh mountain air and savored it before exhaling slowly.

However, his positivity didn't last long.

The trail he was following skirted the base of a misty-peaked mountain, and as he rounded the corner he spotted a small gaggle of figures approaching him. Three in total. Dylan groaned aloud. He wasn't feeling very sociable. In fact, he'd had enough human contact to last him a very long time.

But there was something different about this trio. It was the confident way they carried themselves, and the way they seemed to be at one not just with the sleek, muscular horses they rode, but also with their surroundings. When they drew a little closer Dylan realized that their skin was a few shades darker than even the most hardened settler and they weren't dressed the same way. In fact, two of them were barely dressed at all. A couple of bare-chested men flanked what he could now see was a slender young woman wearing animal skins.

Chumash people.

It was likely Dylan had strayed onto their territory, and there was no way of knowing if they were hostile or not. They had obviously spotted him, probably long before he had seen them, and Dylan didn't want to aggravate the situation by pulling his gun. Any attempt to flee would not only be seen as a sign of weakness, but might be prematurely ended with an arrow or a tomahawk in the back. Besides, he was too tired to run.

He had no choice but to see this one through.

Gripping Skydance between his weary thighs, Dylan held his hands out to the side, palms up, to show that he didn't want any trouble. When they drew close enough to make eye contact, he nodded his head in greeting.

The strangers slowed to a halt.

Oh, no.

One of the trio, a young, well-toned man with white and red warpaint on his face and upper arms, glared back before begrudgingly returning the nod. The other male appeared much older, and what he lacked in warpaint and agility he more than made up for in battle scars that criss-crossed his chest and shoulders. Given how in most native cultures seniority equalled superiority, Dylan took him to be the leader.

The elder Chumash eyed Dylan suspiciously, then turned and said something to the girl riding next to him. She was around twenty years of age and beautiful, petite yet strong looking with a sharp, angled nose and cheekbones set high upon an oval face. When she looked at Dylan, her onyx-black eyes showed no fear, only mild animosity.

"Uncle want know what happen your face," she said, in clipped, heavily-accented English.

For a moment, Dylan was stunned into silence. Then his hand went to his chin. His jaw throbbed and it hurt to speak. But worse than that, he hadn't yet cleaned himself up. His lower face must be covered with dried blood.

"I had a little accident," he replied. "It's fine. No lasting damage."

The girl looked unimpressed. "Why you out here alone?"

"I'm looking for a friend up at Silent Mine. His family haven't heard from him in a while."

The girl said a few words to the older man in Chumash. Dylan assumed she was translating what he had said, and hoped she was doing a good job of it.

The older man nodded sagely but said nothing.

"How..." Dylan began, then stopped, unsure of how to continue.

"How I know your language?"

"Well, yes."

"How you think?" the young woman replied incredulously, "I had teacher. Yo hablo español, tambien. Knowing English and Spanish is good for my people's trade, and it's not 1700 anymore."

"Okay, okay," said Dylan, feeling chastised. "I was just wondering."

Then, the older man started talking, spilling forth a torrent of words.

The young woman took everything in, said a few things back to him, probably for clarification, then looked at Dylan and said curtly, "Uncle think it better you go home."

"Better for me? Or better for him?" Dylan said, instantly suspicious.

"For you. The place you go is dangerous."

"And how is that?"

The young woman paused to find the right words, frowning slightly with concentration. Finally, as if speaking to a small child, she said, "Chumash believe world in three part. Layers? Top, middle, bottom. At top live Sky People, the first ones. The mountains connect their world to middle one. We call it 'Antap. Where we are now. This is 'Antap." The girl swept a slender arm out in front of her dramatically. Then, her face darkened. "Below us is C'oyinahsup. Where monsters live. Our people no belong there. Nor yours."

"I don't plan on going to their world. I'm happy enough in this one, thanks."

"You no understand," the woman said, somehow managing to look both exasperated and bored at the same time. "Some places have... cracks? The cracks let the monsters into our world. What you call Silent Mine is one such place."

"What happens when the monsters come through?"

"They make people like your friend disappear. They take us, too. When I was child my parents tell stories about long ago when ground shook and broke. How you say... earthquake?"

"Sounds 'bout right."

"That night, curtain separating this world and C'oyinahsup was torn, and monsters with no eyes came. There was long, bloody battle, and they slaughter many of my people."

"How did it end?"

"My ancestor force the monster back, at great cost."

"But that's just a story, right?" Dylan said, trying his best to keep the disdain out of his voice. "A legend. Like something your elders would tell kids to make sure they didn't go too far from camp or something?"

"They slaughter my people," the young woman repeated slowly, as if Dylan wasn't quite getting it. "Monsters still there, in C'oyinahsup. They there before humans, and be there after we go. After some time, my people learn to avoid them, and they us. They stay in their world, we stay in ours. When your people come we warn them, but they blinded by riches. All they see is gold. They dig tunnels from our world into C'oyinahsup, and go inside. Into place where monsters with no eyes live."

Dylan wanted to laugh out loud. Not because he found anything the young native woman was telling him especially funny, but because it was a natural reaction to hearing something so fantastic. This was the kind of thing he expected to find in one of his Jules Verne novels, not in real life.

Besides, it was what the settlers did. They took all the old customs, stories, and legends that the indigenous peoples had held dear for countless generations and scoffed, labeling them primitive and simple. Over time, Dylan had slowly come to realize that maybe the settlers were the ignorant ones.

All things considered, his laughter would probably not be appreciated. It might even be construed as disrespectful, and could very well see the Chumash finally losing patience with him. He mustn't forget he was on their turf, and they appeared to be trying to help him, warning him about what might be in store should he continue his journey. They could have let him pass and said nothing.

"I still have to try to find him," Dylan said. "It's my duty. Thanks for your help, and thank your uncle for me. Rest assured, your words are appreciated. I will be careful. I always am."

There was another brief exchange between the young woman and the elder, before she turned to Dylan once more and said, "Uncle wish luck on your quest. And says, 'Remember they too have hearts.'"

"What does that mean?" Dylan asked, bewildered.

"We hope you never find out," the young woman said, turning away and continuing along the path with her two companions.

"Wait!" Dylan called after her. "Do you have a name?"

"Of course," came the curt reply. "What silly question."

But the young woman didn't tell him what it was.

Ask a stupid question, get a stupid answer, Dylan thought and watched the trio of Chumash until they rounded the bend at the base of the mountain and disappeared into the rising sun.

None of them looked back.

-VI-

Dylan was confused by a lot of what the Chumash had said, but more relieved the impromptu meeting had gone smoothly.

Only after he'd resumed his lonely ride did he begin to mull things over. Monsters with no eyes? That sounded terrifying. But what was the significance of having no eyes? Native American folklore was similar to bible stories in the sense that it was full of metaphors and symbolism. Things were often not meant to be taken literally, but were intended to convey some deeper message. It was likely a lot of the meaning in the Chumash stories could have been misinterpreted or lost in translation after countless retellings. 'Monsters' could refer to anything unknown or dangerous, maybe even some of the animals in the area.

But what if, in this case, it was to be taken literally?

What if there really were monsters?

And what if they really didn't have eyes?

They lived underground.

Of course!

It was so dark down there that vision would be useless and if, as the Chumash said, these monsters really were 'as old as the earth,' they would have had plenty of time to adapt and evolve naturally. Perhaps, in the absence of sight, their other senses had become amplified.

Nature had a way of compensating.

When he had been passing through Nebraska, Dylan had met a clairvoyant woman who claimed to have been blind since birth. In her case, what she called her 'sixth' sense had developed far beyond its normal limit and given her the gift of a different kind of sight. She could see things other people couldn't, like the future.

Silent Mine.

The name must also have some significance. By all accounts, the mine was never officially owned by anyone so 'Silent Mine' was more of a colloquial term for something that had no formal name.

Maybe it harked back to the old Chumash tales that other settlers and miners must have heard, and could even be related to these monsters with no eyes. If their other senses had grown to compensate for the absence of vision, maybe their hearing had become dominant. Therefore, it made sense that if you ventured in there, you'd better keep quiet or the so-called monsters would hear you.

Which of course presented an impossible conundrum: how could you mine for gold without making a noise? That was exactly what Sombrero Guy had said before Dylan shot him.

Dylan shivered and made a mental note to be kind to himself in future and think of these things, whatever they were and if they even existed, as creatures rather than monsters. Maybe another race of people or some kind of undiscovered animal, rather than supernatural entities with terrifying powers and unknown qualities. It made them appear more defeatable.

Could that be what the elder had been referring to when he'd said 'they too have hearts?' If they had hearts, they were mortal beings. They could bleed. And if they could bleed, they could be killed.

It was all beginning to make sense, like a real life version of one of those fancy jigsaw puzzles. Dylan could feel his journey coming to an end. Silent Mine must be close now.

If it was where the bartender at Hope's Creek said it was and Dylan stayed on course, he should arrive before noon. The timing was good. Skydance could do with a rest, and he would get one while Dylan explored the mine and surrounding area.

For the first time, he was hit with an almost crippling wave of self-doubt. He could be way out of his depth.

Was he doing the most sensible thing?

Probably not.

Was he doing the *right* thing?

Even that was debatable.

But what else would he be doing? If he wasn't on this job he would probably either be on another one equally as dangerous, or sitting around getting fat somewhere, and there was plenty of time for that. He looked down at his Colt, then at his Winchester stowed in its long scabbard, and suddenly wished he'd invested in more firepower somewhere along the line, or at least stocked up on ammunition at the general store. He had no idea what he might be walking into, and a few bullets might not cut it.

Thumbing a .44 slug out of his gun belt Dylan held it up and examined it, squinting as rays of sunlight reflected off the brass casing. Then he unsheathed his Bowie knife and used it to carve a deep 'X' into the rounded lead tip. This old gunslinger's trick would make the slug fragment upon impact, causing more damage than an ordinary bullet.

As Skydance trudged onwards, he repeated the process five more times, meticulous in his work, then swapped out the ammo in the revolver and replaced it with the newly modified variety. Now he had a whole chamber of rippers. It wasn't much, but it provided an extra level of security and the act kept his mind occupied.

A short while later, he saw a small cluster of cabins in the distance, the harsh right angles making them stand out against the gentle curves of the otherwise unspoiled landscape. There were no straight lines in nature. He couldn't make out any signs of life, but as they approached the small settlement Skydance became increasingly jittery, which was always an indicator of possible trouble. The horse was like an early-warning system.

"It's okay, boy," Dylan said, rubbing the top of Skydance's head. "I think we're almost there."

When they drew closer, Dylan noted the settlement consisted of a row of five one-story wooden shacks and a smaller building set apart from the rest, what he assumed was an outhouse. The buildings looked derelict, but there was a well and several hitching posts in front of them. A lean-to had also been built, probably as a cheaper option than constructing more cabins, with the charred remains of an open fire pit next to it. All in all there was perhaps room to house a dozen men, together with their tools and supplies.

"Hello?" Dylan shouted, surprised at how rough and hoarse his voice sounded. "Anybody here?"

There was no reply, and no movement from any of the shacks.

Dylan cautiously dismounted, tied Skydance to one of the posts, and drew some water from the well. He greedily quenched his thirst, then washed off the blood from his face and the front of his shirt.

Moving slowly and deliberately, he emptied the rest of the bucket over Skydance's head and hindquarters to help cool him down, then filled it again and put it in front of the horse so he could drink. The sun was high in the sky now, so there was little respite. In a few hours it would drop behind the row of shacks. He hoped to be done by then.

Now Dylan could get a closer look at the buildings. The first in the row looked like the oldest, and had long been abandoned. The only window was shattered and the door stood slightly ajar. He edged closer and peered through the opening, breathing a sigh of relief when he discovered it was completely empty save for some litter and a dusty bedroll in the far corner. A pile of splintered wood and debris on the floor where the roof had partially collapsed told him how long the place had stood empty.

The doors of the next two cabins were padlocked, but on looking through the windows Dylan could see even though they were simple one-room affairs, they appeared to be in better condition than the first dwelling and even boasted some basic furnishings in the way of bunk beds, chairs, and tables. Each was equipped with a wood stove, and there were even a few personal touches: a faded photograph stuck on a wall, a cracked shaving mirror. However, they were equally devoid of life.

He wasn't surprised at the basic living conditions. These weren't the kind of places where people came to settle down and raise families. They were working men's cabins. Simple structures designed to provide the most basic amenities for short stints.

Dylan could see the mine now, in all its understated glory. He didn't know what he'd been expecting, but he'd certainly been expecting more than this.

The opening was little more than a crude hole blasted out of the base of the mountain, the jagged edges giving the impression of a mouth opened wide in terror. Large piles of discarded rocks that had been dug out of the ground stood outside like monolithic sentries.

With his hand hovering above the handle of his Colt, Dylan took a few steps closer to the yawning cavern and tried to peer inside.

It was pitch black. Beyond a few feet, he could see nothing.

That was when Dylan realized a fatal flaw in his plan.

He didn't have a lantern.

How was he going to see in there? All he had were a few matches, and they wouldn't last longer than a few minutes. Plus, even he knew how stupid it would be to go into an open mine holding a naked flame. There could be gas.

Cursing his stupidity, he turned his attention to the last of the cabins, which also happened to be the most interesting, now he looked at it. It was smaller than the others, and had no visible windows. Furthermore, it was secured with two padlocks rather than one. All the signs suggested it was more likely used for storage than a living quarters, and there could be something valuable inside the owners wanted to safeguard.

Gold?

No, the miners wouldn't dare keep any gold they scavenged in a communal storeroom, even if it had a double-locked door. All it took to open it, and clean them all out, was someone with a set of keys. Each man would be responsible for his own stash, and would probably keep it with them at all times. When the stash got big enough to be a burden it would be quickly sold, either back at Hope's Creek or maybe to some traveling trader.

So, if not gold, what was inside?

There was only one way to find out.

Dylan trotted back to Skydance, who still had his snout buried in the water bucket, and drew his Winchester. Mindful to keep the barrel pointed away from him should it accidentally discharge, he used the butt of the rifle to batter the padlocks off the door.

They wouldn't break easily, and by the time they lay on the ground amid the dust and chunks of splintered wood, Dylan was sweating and panting with the exertion. When he eventually pulled open the door, he hoped it would be worth the trouble.

He was right. The last shack was indeed a storeroom, and the interior was loaded with supplies and equipment. The first thing he laid eyes on was a double-barrelled shotgun propped against the wall with the barrel sawn off. Dylan snatched up the gun, cracked open the twin barrel and checked to see if it was loaded.

It was.

Why would the miners keep a loaded sawn-off at hand?

When he thought about it, Dylan began to see the logic. Being out here in the middle of nowhere would leave the men susceptible not only to animal attacks but to the attentions of the local Indians. The Chumash Dylan had met were friendly, but they might be the exception to the rule. There might be other, more aggressive tribes in the area and there was always the threat of bandits. The miners probably didn't want to be weighed down with an arsenal and probably didn't even carry sidearms, so it made sense to have some form of protection on site.

But the fact the barrel had been sawn off didn't sit well with him. It indicated strongly that any trouble the miners had been expecting was likely to be up close and personal.

Dylan shoved the weapon into his belt. He hoped he wouldn't have to use it, but might be glad of the extra firepower before the day was out. He quickly scanned the cabin for more cartridges, but came up short. The supplies had been arranged to leave a narrow passage through the middle, presumably to allow access to items at the back without having to pull everything out. Cautiously, Dylan entered the unlit space, almost bumping his head on something hanging from a rack fixed to the ceiling.

Lanterns.

Yes!

There was one problem solved. Perhaps his luck was about to change. Selecting a lantern, he took it down and checked it. It was over half full of kerosene and appeared to be in pretty good shape, so he lighted the wick and stood back in admiration as the soft yellow light filled the confined space. That would do nicely.

The cabin was filled with what you might expect to find: sturdy wooden bracing posts were stacked high, along with various tools and crates. Holding the lantern above his head, he opened one of the crates and looked inside. It was filled with sticks of dynamite packed in sawdust. The kind with a fuse you lit.

Looking around, Dylan saw it wasn't just one case of dynamite, but at least seven or eight. The miners must have been using it to blast through the rock. He couldn't believe there was so much of it. Dynamite was valuable, and not the kind of thing you just left behind when you moved on, unless you expected to be coming back soon.

Or were forced to leave in a hurry.

He also found boxes of chalk, both red and white, that must have been used for marking things out. Thinking it was something else that may come in handy, he stuffed a handful in his pocket.

Exiting the storage shed, Dylan closed the door behind him and wedged it shut. He suddenly regretted smashing the locks off. That dynamite had probably been paid for by the miners, and now anybody could go in and take it. He decided to report it to the sheriff when he got back to Hope's Creek, so he could arrange to get new locks put on the door. But perhaps he would leave out the part where it was actually him who damaged them in the first place.

In the meantime, there was work to do.

Finding no sign of Thomas Winstanley at the camp could mean only one thing: if he was here at all, he was inside the mine.

The sun was now directly overhead, meaning it was early afternoon. He should be thinking about his next meal by now, but he couldn't bring himself to feel hungry. There was a time and a place for everything. This might be the time, but it wasn't the place. He wanted to be well away from Silent Mine before night fell. He didn't want to admit as much, but the place gave him the creeps, and he didn't want to be there after dark.

He eyed the rough hole in the base of the mountain once more, and doubt settled over him like a heavy woolen blanket. Common sense, and it felt like every other sense he had, was imploring him to leave. To forget finding Thomas Winstanley, take Skydance, and get the hell out of there.

But the overriding feeling was one of inquisitiveness. If there were secrets here, he wanted to know what they were. He also had a strong sense of duty. Thomas Winstanley's family deserved to know what had happened to him, or at least whether he was here or not. Finally, of course, there was the vague promise of riches, which he was fully aware had led many men to their doom. Dylan could claim his intentions were noble all he wanted, but would be lying if the lure of finding gold up there wasn't a contributing factor in his decision making.

It all added up to the fact that if Dylan left without exploring the mine he would be sorry, and he was someone who would much rather regret something he did than something he didn't do. He picked up his Winchester from where he'd left it propped against the storage cabin, savoring its comforting weight.

Now he had another decision to make.

He would certainly appreciate the security the rifle provided. But it was heavy and unwieldy, and for effective use required both hands. That wouldn't be practical in a confined space, especially if one of his hands happened to be holding a lantern, which would arguably be of more importance in the darkness than any firearm. He looked down at the borrowed sawn-off shotgun in his belt and his Colt in its holster, and decided that would be enough. Somewhat reluctantly, he went over to Skydance, gave him a pat, and put the Winchester back in its long-holster. What was he expecting to find in there, anyway, monsters?

It was ridiculous. Crazy Indian talk. They exaggerated everything. It was in their nature. Either that or they plain made up stories just to keep white folks off their land.

He couldn't help wondering if the three Chumash had a good laugh at his expense after they'd parted ways. Well, he thought, let's see how much they laughed when they realized their outlandish tales and stern warnings had no effect on him.

Dylan took a deep breath, steadied himself, lighted his kerosene lantern, and entered the mine.

-VII-

The moment the darkness engulfed him, the atmosphere changed and Dylan found himself battling a mild case of claustrophobia. The area immediately beyond the entrance was a bulbous shape and more expansive than he had imagined. But the ceiling was so low he had to stoop, and there were scrapes and chisel marks on the walls giving the unsettling impression that people had been trying to dig their way out rather than in.

He was suddenly glad he'd had the good fortune to find the lantern.

After the cavernous opening section, the mine narrowed into a more typical shaft leading on a slight downward trajectory deeper into the mountain. After a last lingering look at the sunlight streaming through the entrance behind him, Dylan stepped into the shaft.

Immediately, he noticed how much cooler the air was inside. It was also damp and clammy, the moisture clinging to his skin like sweat.

Suddenly, he felt something brush his face, and recoiled in horror before realizing it was just a spider's web. The ceiling of the shaft was a few inches lower than the entrance, and the walls were barely three feet apart, making moving with any freedom difficult. At times the walls narrowed so much that Dylan had to hold his breath and squeeze his broad shoulders through. Wooden posts had been placed at irregular intervals to stop the roof from collapsing, and Dylan could only hope they held out.

The ground underfoot was hard, uneven and pebble strewn. Judging by the shape of the shaft, it appeared to have once been a crack or void forming part of a network of subterranean caves and passages under the earth's crust like veins beneath skin. Over the years this particular section had been painstakingly chiseled out or blasted away by a succession of workers until it reached its current state.

The absence of a tram track pointed to the relatively small scale of the operation and meant the rock had to have been manually taken outside and dumped by hand. So much heavy, dangerous work for not much reward.

Dylan had met gold miners on his travels before, and while they all liked to embellish and claim they had a lot more luck than they really did, he knew most of them lived hand-to-mouth and could go days or weeks without making a cent. It was a hard life, filled with peril. That was why when they struck lucky, they had to strike hard.

Remembering the chalk in his pocket, he hastily scribbled a marker on the nearest wall. The last thing he needed was to get lost underground. If the worst came to the worst, he could just follow the trail back out.

It was beginning to smell bad. When he'd first entered, the air had been stuffy and stale with an underlying odor of damp. But as he ventured farther into the mine, Dylan began to detect a more pervasive, unpleasant smell that was getting progressively worse. Putrid, pungent and vaguely fruity, it was the unmistakable stench of decay. Rotting flesh. An animal must have found its way inside and died. A big animal.

At least, he hoped that was the case.

Suddenly, by the flickering yellow light of the lantern, he saw movement in front of him. It was there for a fraction of a second, then it was gone.

Dylan froze and held his breath, eyes searching the shadows. Then he breathed a heavy sigh of relief mixed with repulsion when a fat, fearless rat emerged from the darkness, sniffed at the air not two feet from Dylan's boots, and retreated back where it came from.

He turned and craned his neck to look behind him. The entrance to the mine, and the freedom it represented, was now no more than a thin sliver of white light. It wouldn't be long before it disappeared altogether.

Marking the wall again, he paused to compose himself and debate whether to press on or turn around, when for an instant the sliver of white light was suddenly obscured.

What the hell?

Assuming his mind wasn't already playing tricks, it could mean one of only two things: either something had passed by the opening outside, or something was in the mine shaft with him.

Before he could stop himself, or even think about what he was doing, he bellowed, "Hello? Anyone there?"

The moment the words passed his lips he regretted it. Not only did speaking send bolts of pain through his injured jaw, but anything or anyone in the mine would certainly have heard him. Now, he'd lost the element of surprise, and any faint hope he'd been harboring of getting in and out undiscovered evaporated. All he could do now was try to turn the situation to his advantage by asserting himself. With nothing left to lose, he called out again, "Mister Thomas Winstanley, are you in here?"

The question echoed around the shaft then faded away, leaving nothing in its wake but a thick silence broken only by the almost imperceptible plink-plonk of water dripping somewhere.

Dylan held the lantern out behind him in an effort to extend his field of vision as far as he could. Nothing entered its sacred arc of light.

He was beginning to think he must have imagined the movement after all, and prepared himself to push on.

Suddenly, the fragile stillness was shattered by a shrill, high-pitched howl. Or it might have been a scream.

At first it was impossible to tell whether the vocalization was made by an animal or a human. He couldn't even tell whether the noise was friendly or hostile as it seemed to contain no element of pain or distress. If anything, it sounded calculated. Almost like a rallying call.

The sound made Dylan's blood run cold. He hadn't been mistaken. There was something in the shaft behind him.

The sheer emotion of it all was too much: the sense of being alone and alienated, cut off from civilization, trapped in a confined space and in a potentially dangerous situation with no safety net all melted together to give Dylan's brain one instruction.

Run.

He broke into a desperate, shambling trot, the only thing in his mind being to put some distance between him and whatever had made that noise. He had no idea what lay in front of him. All he knew was he would rather face the unknown than turn around and tackle whatever was behind him.

Scraping his elbows and bumping his head, he ricocheted off the unforgiving walls as he propelled himself forward. At one point he came to a mini cave-in blocking half the shaft and had to squeeze past while panic threatened to consume him. Once free, he stumbled and fell to his knees, holding onto the lantern for all he was worth.

Then, he was up again and pushing forward.

Soon, he came to a fork in the shaft, the passage splitting into two tunnels of roughly equal dimensions.

Left or right?

Without pausing too long to think about it, Dylan scrawled a chalk mark on the wall and ducked into the right-hand shaft, which appeared slightly wider and more accommodating.

As he scrambled onward he was plagued by the feeling that someone or something was just out of sight behind him, snapping at his heels. The sensation was so strong, several times Dylan was compelled to turn and look. Each time, he could have sworn he glimpsed movement before whatever it was melted back into the shadows.

Despite his adrenaline-fueled terror, Dylan soon began to slow, the muscles in his arms and legs burning as exhaustion set in. Deciding to use the last of his energy to make a stand, he crouched in the narrow passageway, put the lantern on the floor in front of him, drew his Colt, and pointed it into the darkness, expecting to be rushed at any moment.

But only the sound of his labored breathing and thudding heartbeat filled the shaft. There was nothing pursuing him. Could he have been mistaken?

Shifting his attention to the front, Dylan strained to peer into the inky blackness. Nothing stirred there, either.

Regardless, it was clear he'd outstayed his welcome at Silent Mine and needed to get out.

Now he was faced with another difficult decision: should he try to retrace his steps back to the entrance or keep going and hope to find a quicker way out?

Examining the walls of the passage he found himself in, he noticed that they didn't appear to be tooled and there were no wooden supports. That indicated he was in a part of the mine that had not been excavated. It might not even have been explored. At some point, the shaft must have intersected with a natural cave formation.

Most caves and fissures eventually found their way into the open, didn't they? He seemed to remember someone telling him that, and hoped it was true.

It was a gamble. But even with the chalk marks, he wasn't confident in being able to find his way out if he turned back. In the dim light the marks would be easy to miss, plus there were long stretches where he hadn't used any chalk at all. He remembered navigating one intersection, but had there been more? Furthermore, he wasn't entirely convinced he wasn't being stalked. Or by what.

Keeping his Colt drawn and gripping the lantern tighter than ever with his other hand, Dylan took a deep breath, composed himself, and continued on into uncharted territory. There was no denying it, the deeper into the subterranean system he ventured, the stronger the smell of rotting flesh became. Before long it was almost overpowering, and he was forced to tie his bandanna around the lower half of his face to keep out the stench. It made little difference.

That was when the scream, or the howl, came again.

This time, it sounded closer. So close it could almost have come from directly behind him.

Cocking the Colt with his thumb, Dylan whirled around and pointed it into the cluster of shadows immediately behind him.

Again, he saw something move.

Or thought he did.

Between the poor light quality and the speed at which it happened, it was impossible to make out any detail or even estimate how big or far away it was. But whatever he was dealing with moved with all the lithe dexterity of an alley cat.

Seeing it again, even if only fleetingly, and again hearing the blood-curdling sound it made, convinced Dylan of one thing: it wasn't human.

Without giving himself time to think, he fired the Colt.

He didn't even aim. There was nothing to aim at, except the darkness itself. His intention was more to scare away whatever was on his trail than kill it.

A burst of fire erupted from the gun's muzzle and in the confined space, the noise was louder than he ever thought possible. The deafening roar made his ears ring and reverberated around the solid stone walls again and again. It was like being caught in a war zone.

Much like when he had verbally challenged his pursuer, the moment he pulled the trigger, he regretted it. It was an impulsive reaction, fueled by fear and confusion. Sure, the noise might scare away any predators within earshot, but it also let anyone and anything within the mine know where he was. If they didn't know already.

Cursing his own stupidity, Dylan started moving again at pace. He had no choice now but to move to a new location before whatever the gunshot might have attracted arrived.

He didn't get very far.

Another sound came from behind him, stopping him in his tracks. This wasn't a scream or a howl; it sounded like a rock being tossed.

What the heck?

That could only mean that whatever was in here with him was intelligent, and either fixing to attack him or trying to get his attention.

As Dylan tried desperately to get everything that was happening straight in his mind, he saw the creature for the first time. And he was right.

It wasn't human.

Far from it.

Though it was humanoid in appearance, what he saw was smaller than the average person. No more than three feet tall. And as it bounded through the tunnel, leaped, and launched itself at him, Dylan thought he was being attacked by something straight out of a fairytale.

Or a nightmare.

His brain, already stretched to breaking point, had only a moment to register what he was seeing as the creature passed through the small arc of light cast by the lantern and disappeared into the darkness. It was skinny and pale, and covered in wrinkled skin with patches of what looked like coarse black fur. The last thing that registered before the thing pounced and landed on him, pushing him to the ground as it clawed at his face and neck, was that the Chumash stories were true.

The creature had no eyes.

-VIII-

When the creature threw itself at him, both the Colt and the lantern were knocked out of Dylan's grasp and fell to the floor. Miraculously, the lantern didn't break. That would have been disastrous. Instead it lay on its side, providing more than enough light for him to see what he was fighting.

He didn't know if that was a blessing or a curse.

The creature sitting on him had prominent, concave ears protruding from the sides of its head and a long, tapered nose. Its face was dominated by a thin-lipped mouth, opened wide to reveal an untidy mess of pointed, blackened teeth. All in all, the creature had a horrific, gnome-like appearance.

Its pale skin was streaked with dirt and grime, and it blew hot, stale air onto Dylan's face as they wrestled, making him gag at the fetid, foul-smelling odor. The nightmarish creature emitted a low keening sound as it forced its mouth closer and closer to the exposed skin of Dylan's neck like a lover trying to plant a kiss.

Dylan lashed out with his fist, connecting with the side of the creature's head several times, but the blows seemed to have no effect. Being in such a compromised position, he couldn't generate enough power to do any real damage. Instead, he gripped hold of the thing's lower jaw and worked to get his hand under its chin in an effort to push it off.

The creature was ferocious, its sinewy strength belying its small stature.

Quick as a flash, its head snapped to the opposite side and it chomped at the air inches from Dylan's throat.

As a last resort, he thrust out his hand and rammed it inside the creature's gaping mouth. It gleefully bit down, and Dylan threw back his head and screamed as twin sets of razor-like incisors sliced through skin and flesh.

Despite the pain, he didn't let go, sensing that if he did, he would be a dead man. Instead, he held the creature's lower jaw as tightly as he could with his wounded hand and simultaneously brought his stronger right hand in a sweeping motion to grip its upper jaw and nose. Then, he yanked in opposing directions as hard as he could.

The creature's lower jaw dislocated with an audible snap and the skin at the corners of its mouth ripped open, dousing Dylan's hand and wrist with warm, viscous fluid that looked black in the limited light. The creature spluttered and let out another of those high-pitched wails. This one, however, was filled with pain.

Spurred by seeing his actions were hurting the creature, Dylan didn't stop pushing and pulling until finally, the lower jaw separated from the creature's face altogether with an awful, wet tearing sound.

A deluge of gore cascaded over Dylan's face and chest. Throwing the detached jaw aside, he finally succeeded in using his hips to flip the wounded creature off him and turn so he was on top. Utilizing his considerable body weight, he pinned the thrashing form to the ground, turning his head away in revulsion as his fingers sank into the damp, clammy skin of its throat.

He didn't know what it was, but he knew this thing was dangerous. Lethal, even. Like a spooked rattlesnake or a cornered wolf, if he didn't finish it off, it was probably going to do its best to kill him.

Dylan scanned the immediate area for the Colt he had dropped.

Where the hell was it?

In the reduced visibility, he couldn't see anything.

The gun must have landed somewhere beyond the arc of the lantern's light. He felt the weight of the sawn-off he'd liberated from the storage shack in his waistband, but wasn't sure if he could trust it. Damn. Why hadn't he tested it? He thought fleetingly about going for the Derringer in his boot, but couldn't manipulate his body enough to make a grab for it. His top priority was keeping this gurgling, writhing creature under control. Even if it was injured, he couldn't risk letting it go for even a second. There was no telling what it might do. Lurking beneath all these considerations was the simple fact that he was afraid discharging a gun in the tunnel would bring the roof down on him.

The only other weapon within easy reach was his Bowie knife.

Holding the creature in place with one hand, he quickly drew the knife from its scabbard. The blade glinted in the lantern's light as he raised it high in the air then brought it down into the creature's face where it glanced off its cheekbone, opening a deep gash in its cheek.

It howled again and thrashed even harder, its supple body jerking and squirming as if in the throes of a convulsion.

Dylan stabbed at it again, instinctively aiming for where its eyes should be, hoping to find some kind of weak spot. But as sharp as the knife was, it wasn't able to penetrate deep enough into the thing's face to do much damage. It was as if its face and head were covered with a thick veneer.

Adjusting his body position, Dylan switched his attention instead to the creature's unprotected throat and drove the knife in again. This time, he felt a rush of euphoria when, after only minimal resistance, it slid in to the hilt.

He twisted the blade, pulled it out, and repeated the action over and over again until the creature lay motionless in a spreading pool of foul black liquid, its head virtually decapitated.

Exhausted and drained, Dylan rolled onto his back to catch his breath, turning his head to get a closer look at the creature.

What the hell are you?

With its sprightly frame, pronounced ears and nose and lack of eyes, it seemed specifically designed to function underground in complete darkness.

Then a thought struck him like a punch to the gut.

There wouldn't be just one.

These things lived down here, procreating and multiplying, and had done for hundreds or thousands of years. Who knew how many of them might be crawling around in this subterranean network of passages? This was their domain, and Dylan was the interloper.

The species probably subsisted on whatever they could find underground: bats, frogs, rats and other vermin, fungi, insects, maybe even each other. No doubt their diet was supplemented by larger animals that strayed into the tunnels, and even the miners who came to plunder the caves for gold. Perhaps, in times of desperation and under cover of darkness, the creatures even ventured outside to hunt.

The Chumash story now made a little more sense. The earthquake referenced in their folklore had torn a hole in the mountainside, which they saw as a veil separating two worlds, allowing these creatures to spill forth in search of food.

The creatures probably hadn't learned to distinguish men from animals, so they attacked both with gay abandon. If that were the case, it must have been a steep learning curve culminating in the harsh truth that men could fight back. And most of them had weapons.

Just then, another dark thought struck him. He was well read enough to know that fairytales about little folk making people disappear permeated every major culture in the world, including that of the local native Americans.

His family was from Wales, where stories about tylwyth teg, or the "fair family" were rife. There was even a variety of little person, or fairy, called the Coblynau that were said to exclusively populate mines. Generally speaking, they stayed out of sight, only making their presence known through knocking, which they used to communicate. This gave rise to them becoming known as "Knockers" in other parts of Britain, and they were an accepted part of life in the mines.

Dylan looked again at the dead thing lying on the ground. Could it be a real-life example of a Coblynau? A Knocker?

Perhaps these things were everywhere, not just living beneath the surface of every country and continent, but thriving. Mining of any description was a notoriously dangerous occupation. There were accidents aplenty, and people went missing, presumed dead, all the time. What if these creatures were responsible for some of those tragedies? How many battles had taken place deep underground that nobody had survived? Even if someone did live to tell the tale, they would be ridiculed for their trouble, and might decide it was in their best interests to make up some other, more plausible cover story. A gas explosion or a cave-in.

Dylan glanced down at his wounded hand. His pinky finger was broken, and stuck out at an unnatural angle. Apart from that, there were several deep cuts where the creature's teeth had ripped to the bone. Now that the adrenaline was wearing off, the pain was coming in waves. Wincing, he pulled off his bandanna and wrapped it around his hand to stem the bleeding. Thank God he'd had the presence of mind to stick his left hand in the thing's mouth rather than his right, or else he really would be compromised. At least with only his left hand damaged he could still use his gun.

Just as he was preparing to get moving again, he heard the first knock. Three quick raps, almost like someone asking to be let in. With the way the sound echoed around the chamber, it was difficult to tell where it was coming from, but Dylan's instinct told him it must have originated some distance away.

He was still trying to process the concept that another of the creatures was nearby when the knocks were answered by another set, these a lot closer. Again, there were three raps, but this time they were quicker and sharper, with a longer gap between the second and third knocks.

Then there were more. A sequence of two this time. It almost sounded as if there were groups of the things in different parts of the mine communicating with each other.

Dylan's mouth suddenly went dry. If he hadn't been in a bad spot before, he was now.

He had to get the hell out of the mine. Fast. But it seemed as if whichever direction he went, he would run into more of these things with no eyes. His firepower would help. They might be resistant to knife blades, but it would be interesting to see how resistant they were to modified .45 ripper slugs.

Snatching the gun up off the ground, he opened the chamber and replaced the bullet he had fired. Now he was fully loaded.

The knocks and raps continued. Three more, answered by another set. These sounded a long way distant. Soon, there was a cacophony of noise coming from all around, both faint and loud, near and far.

Dylan covered his ears with his hands to keep out the noise and grimaced. It was overwhelming. How many creatures were there? A dozen? A hundred? A thousand? Were there as many of these things beneath the surface of the earth as there were people living on it? Did they have actual functioning communities down here? Underground cities?

And then, as if on some signal, the chorus of knocks stopped, plunging the mine into a deep stillness. Even the air felt leaden and heavy. The sudden impenetrable silence was even more disconcerting than the noise.

If he was going to run into more of these things, he planned to be ready this time. Holding the lantern in his bandaged left hand and the Colt, cocked and ready, in his right, Dylan slowly ventured farther along the passage. The last thing he wanted to do was spend the night in the mine, so he wrinkled his nose against the stench, fought to control his breathing, increased his pace and began praying for a chink of light.

On the way, he passed numerous other tunnels branching off the one he was in. Most of them were too small to accommodate a full-grown man, and common sense decreed that he would be better off sticking to what appeared to be a main passageway. Sacrificing the extra insurance for speed, he refrained from marking his way with chalk.

Regardless of size, Dylan passed each opening warily, mindful of something lying in wait and jumping out at him. He made steady progress, until something that looked out of place caught his eye.

It was a piece of tattered, light-blue cloth, perhaps two inches square, stuck to a piece of rock jutting out of the wall at knee height. It looked to have been torn from someone's clothing, suggesting at some time, someone else must have been here. The thought both reassured Dylan and filled him with dread.

So he wasn't the first human to venture this far.

But what had happened to his predecessor?

Immediately beyond the piece of cloth was another narrow opening leading off the main passage. This was significant, Dylan could sense it, and the powerful stench spilling out of the void only underscored the notion. It seemed as though he'd found the source of the foul, meaty stink permeating the cave system.

The ceiling was lower here, forcing Dylan to stoop even lower to get inside. After what had transpired so far, he didn't think anything else he encountered could surprise him.

How wrong he was.

The crude, narrow opening fed into a large cavity that finally allowed Dylan to stand up and flex his back. By the flickering light of the lantern, the first thing he saw was a figure slumped against the far wall.

Breath catching in his throat, he thrust the Colt in the direction of the threat, only to find there was no threat at all.

He was looking at a long-dead corpse, decomposed and stripped of flesh to such an extent it was really more of a rag-covered skeleton. The chest and stomach had been viciously torn open as if something wanted to get at the succulent goodies inside, the withered skin framing the wound peeled back like old yellowing paper.

When Dylan peered closer, he saw the remaining patches of skin were peppered with what looked like bites, and the exposed bones of the poor unfortunate's face were covered in abrasions and teeth marks. Either the rats or those things, the monsters with no eyes, had been feasting on it.

Dylan again felt like throwing up, and had to cover his mouth to stop himself doing so. He needed some water, and reminded himself next time he agreed to enter a deserted gold mine in the middle of nowhere crawling with inhuman freaks, to be sure to bring some.

Something twinkled through the gaps in the desiccated fingers.

Retching in his throat as the digits popped and cracked, Dylan gently prised them open. There, lying in the dead man's palm, were two gold nuggets, each as big as his thumbnail. The miner must have been holding them when he died and refused to let them go. Having given his life in pursuit of it, he wasn't going to give up his prize, even in death.

Dylan felt a brief stab of guilt when he took the pair of nuggets and dropped them in his pocket, but the miner had no use for them. If Dylan didn't take them, they would lie there forever. Or at least until someone else came along.

Something at the edge of the shadows caught his attention. He slowly swung the lamp around, and his horror was magnified as he looked around the chamber and realized it didn't contain just one body.

The corpses were piled high, dozens of them in varying states of decay and consumption, stacked on top of each other like slabs of meat in a butcher shop. No wonder the smell was so bad. It appeared Dylan had stumbled across the creatures' larder.

Was Thomas Winstanley among the poor souls?

Maybe.

Maybe not.

And that would have to be good enough for anyone who asked, because Dylan didn't plan on searching through the bodies.

He'd seen enough.

-IX-

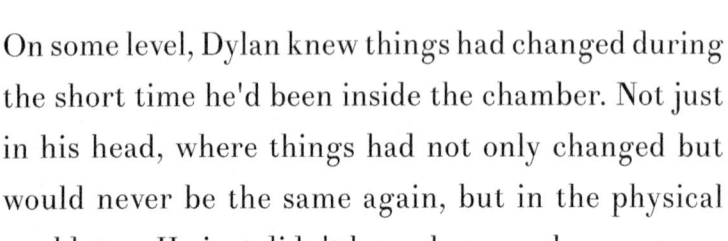

On some level, Dylan knew things had changed during the short time he'd been inside the chamber. Not just in his head, where things had not only changed but would never be the same again, but in the physical world, too. He just didn't know how much.

When he emerged from what he would later remember as "the larder," it was like stepping into hell. Gnomes, Coblynau, Knockers, monsters with no eyes, whatever they were, swarmed everywhere. Too many to count, they clambered over the walls and over each other, heads cocked, lithe, pale limbs twitching feverishly.

The sensation was akin to biting into an apple and finding a nest of maggots inside.

Dylan's spirits sank. He was hopelessly outnumbered, and there were far too many to fight. As much as he loathed the thought, he couldn't see any other outcome than him being the next body stacked atop the pile. But even with his fate all but decided, he wasn't going down easily.

He was going to give them a fight they'd never forget.

As he looked around he realized that they hadn't zeroed in on him yet, but they'd come looking for him en mass guided by the commotion he'd caused. The cacophony of knocking he had heard was a call to arms, or their equivalent of "dinner is ready."

As if his situation wasn't perilous enough, he was now faced with an impossible choice. Should he try to retrace his steps or go deeper into the mine and hope to stumble across a different way out? He decided he would have a marginally better chance of surviving the first option, but it was clear he was going to have to blast his way out. But the moment he fired the first shot, the noise would give away his position and they would be on him. The only solution was to try to weave his way through the writhing mass of entwined bodies making no noise, creating as little disturbance as possible, and hoping the creatures somehow remained oblivious to his presence.

Of course, that wouldn't solve the underlying problem of being lost in the mine, but he could only tackle challenges one at a time and his most immediate concern revolved around getting away from this particular section of the tunnel system without being slaughtered and eaten.

The width of the passage, narrow in the best of circumstances, was made even more restrictive by the presence of the creatures. Holding his breath, Dylan turned sideways and tried to work his body through the tiny gaps in the squirming mass. Rising above the fruity stench of rotting flesh was the sour stink of sweat. He could hear the creatures breathing, and some were making a low, keening noise.

He needed to look all around him at once, not least down at the floor, where even the slightest trip or scuff of the boot could betray him.

It was slow going, Dylan's frayed nerves stretching to unimaginable lengths as he inched his way forward with a sequence of exaggerated movements as if he was some kind of crazed mime artist.

It was all going so well, until it wasn't.

As is so often the case in life, a complete, irreversible change in fortunes was brought about by the most trivial, everyday thing. A single, momentary lapse of concentration.

A spider. An arachnid not even big enough to startle a child, but big enough to make Dylan give an involuntary snort of surprise when it dropped onto his cheek. The tiny, innocuous noise was enough to alert every creature in the passage, and seemingly as one, they opened their mouths to reveal those awful, sharp teeth.

Giving up on his perverse pantomime, he broke into a loping sprint, knocking pale, emaciated bodies from their purchases and trampling them underfoot as tiny clawed hands grasped at his clothes.

One, two, three, were clinging onto his legs, slowing him down, while another attached itself to his back. Dylan screamed as a white-hot bolt of pain seared through his shoulder.

It was biting him. Trying to eat him alive.

Using the revolver as a bludgeoning tool, he contorted his upper body and battered at the creature until it dropped off him. Now, he had nothing to lose by shooting. Still on the move, Dylan pointed the Colt at one of the pale forms in front of him and pulled the trigger.

An explosion-like roar echoed in the tunnel, and a blinding flash momentarily illuminated proceedings. There was a split second of stunned silence, then came the cacophony of screeches. It sounded as if the creatures were in physical pain. This idea was reinforced by their obvious disorientation. They scattered, presumably in a bid to get away from the source of the noise, but confusion reigned and most of them collided with each other.

The shot Dylan fired missed its target, but struck the creature next to it just above the elbow. The modified bullet did its job and shattered on impact, blowing off the creature's lower arm. It threw back its head and let out a wail as streams of black liquid spurted geyser like from the newly formed stump.

As the gunshot's echo began to fade, the wall of creatures melted away, clearing a path of sorts. Ignoring the pain in his shoulder, Dylan put his head down and plowed on.

Something whizzed past his head and clattered on the ground in front of him. A rock. He felt a stinging pain as another struck him between his shoulder blades. They were trying to stone him.

It's how they hunt.

Suddenly, one of the creatures loomed out of the darkness directly in front of him, opening its mouth and baring its sharp, too-big teeth.

Without breaking stride, Dylan aimed the revolver and fired, hitting the creature between the eyes. Under the circumstances, it was a good shot, and he expected to see the gormless creature's head explode in a foul mist of blood and brains.

But to his astonishment, modified or not, the bullet bounced off the creature's toughened skull, and succeeded only in putting it down just long enough for Dylan to skirt past it.

Two hits, and zero kills. If he was going to get out of this, he needed to drastically improve his strike rate. He remembered how difficult it had been to drive a knife into the head of the first creature that had attacked him, reinforcing the idea that their heads must be protected by some kind of natural armor. Perhaps it was the way they had evolved down here, where the perpetual darkness meant eyes were useless as a form of defense and falling debris was a constant threat.

Moments after he fired the shots, the hordes regrouped and were advancing on him again. They seemed to be everywhere at once: the walls, the floor, the ceiling. Hundreds of them, seething and undulating as if they were one big, amorphous organism.

As Dylan fought his way through he was suddenly struck by an unsettling, surreal thought so powerful it was almost a flashback. This experience, fighting his way through a constricted tunnel, was like passing through his mother's cervix on the way to being born. The biggest differences being that back then, he wasn't being attacked from all sides and there would have been a light at the end of the tunnel.

How appropriate that should he die here; these two similarly intense experiences, so full of fear, angst, and uncertainty, would book-end his life.

The irony wasn't lost on him.

He was forced to swivel on his heels to kick out at a creature steadfastly clinging to his trouser leg, stumbled, lost his balance and then over-compensated before finally correcting himself.

That was a close call. Too close. If he went to ground, they would swarm and overpower him within seconds, ensuring he never got up again.

Another small pebble bounced off his buttocks.

Then he realized he was still carrying the sawed-off shotgun. If these things thought his Colt was noisy, the shotgun would be on a different level and might also do more damage. Especially at close range.

Silently bemoaning the fact that he only had two hands to work with, he reluctantly holstered the still-smoking Colt and drew the shotgun from his belt. It was heavier than the revolver, feeling more sturdy and powerful. He aimed, and squeezed one of the triggers.

BOOM!

The eruption of light and sound was so powerful Dylan's first thought was that he'd made yet another tactical error. It seemed loud enough to bring the roof down. Thankfully, it didn't happen. But confronted with red-hot buckshot, the creatures shrank into the shadows once more, shielding their ears with their hands. The discharge combined with the unanticipated force of the recoil almost sent Dylan reeling, too. But after a slight wobble he maintained momentum and kept moving forward.

A few seconds later, when the tunnel of writhing bodies threatened to close around him again, he fired the other barrel into the throng to give himself another moment's respite. Then, lungs burning and limbs heavy, he threw the empty shotgun to the ground. He was out of cartridges. The gun was useless to him now and its weight would only slow him down.

The cards were almost dealt, and the situation had a growing sense of inevitability about it. Dylan began to think that by continuing to fight he was just prolonging the agony. He was alone, trapped, and running out of options and ammunition, not to mention luck.

With his undamaged hand, he gave himself a sharp slap across the face. Negative thoughts were more dangerous than any physical enemy. He had to get a hold of himself.

The slap had the desired effect and Dylan immediately got his second wind. He wasn't ready to just lie down and die. Not yet. There was still so much to do.

But the seething mob was closing in. They leapt at him from the walls, forcing him into taking ungainly sidesteps to evade them, and he could literally feel them breathing down the back of his neck. The stones they threw bounced and clattered around the tunnel, some hitting him and some missing, but all adding to the mayhem.

Just when he began to think all hope was lost, the unthinkable happened.

Something whistled past his face from the other direction. The direction he was running. Even above the cacophony of noise and excitement he distinctly heard the soft whoosh and felt the displacement of air on his cheek.

Maybe on some level, he recognized it for what it was, but it didn't immediately register. There was simply too much going on for him to process everything. It felt as if his senses were being overwhelmed and he was sinking beneath the weight of it all. He had to prioritize, listen to his instincts, and they told him to keep running.

The next time it happened, he was dimly aware of something crossing his line of vision, only to be gone without a trace a moment later.

There was a thud and a pained squawk somewhere behind him. Whatever was going on seemed to be causing some disruption. Dylan wanted to turn around to look. It might help him understand the situation. But he knew if he did, he might lose his footing, and that would spell the end. He couldn't take the risk, and had to concentrate on making the most of any advantage that came his way, however miniscule.

One of the creatures must have been lying in wait, and leapt out at Dylan from the shadows with a manic screech. He swatted it away and saw it hit the nearest wall out of the corner of his eye. That punch had taken out ranchers bigger and heavier than him before. It was more than enough to put down a three-foot gargoyle.

But he couldn't punch all of them.

Now, focused only on carrying the lantern and not falling over, he had more freedom of movement and began to finally make some ground.

Another whistling sound, and again confusion reigned in the space directly behind him.

Just as Dylan's overstretched mind was beginning to comprehend what was going on, a female voice cut through the darkness. "This way!"

At first, Dylan wasn't concerned about who the voice belonged to. He was just happy to know he wasn't alone after all. As he rode the sudden wave of elation, he finally worked out what that whooshing noise he kept hearing was.

Arrows.

Someone was firing arrows over his shoulders into the horde chasing him, missing him by inches each time. Right on cue, another whistled past his right ear.

"Hurry!" the voice urged.

Dylan poured every ounce of energy he had into putting more distance between him and the creatures. He didn't care where he was going or who he was running to. The fact that the voice was human was all he needed to know.

"Use your guns! Aim for their hearts!"

Dylan's mind flashed back to his meeting with the Chumash.

Remember they too have hearts.

Now, it finally made sense. After finding out they had armored skulls, the Chumash had worked out the easiest way to kill these things was by shooting them in the heart.

Dylan drew his Colt, turned on a dime, and ran backward while he emptied the revolver into the creatures rushing up behind him. Taking the mystery voice's advice, he lowered his aim, and saw the two at the front of the pack propelled backward by the force of the .44 slugs. He had a feeling they wouldn't be getting up. Satisfyingly, as they careered backward, they tripped up some of those following too close behind like bowling balls.

He inwardly cheered at seeing an arrow take out another, lodging itself deep in the chest of the onrushing creature. It was an impressive shot at a moving target, though the creature's forward momentum probably didn't help its cause. It must have been like running headlong into an oversized nail.

By the flickering light of the lantern, Dylan began to make out a slender figure crouching in the passage ahead of him. He drew back the empty Colt to pistol whip it before realizing he wasn't looking at another creature. It was the Chumash girl he had met on the trail. The one who'd declined to tell him her name.

She was working her bow with practiced ease and loosed off another arrow as he approached, the projectile sailing past him into some unknown target. She was laying down cover to enable him to make his escape, and doing an excellent job of it.

"Keep running!" she yelled as he drew within a few feet of her. "Go straight!"

Dylan did as he was instructed, tucking the lantern under his arm and taking the opportunity to reload. He had run out of rippers. But now that he knew how to kill them, it shouldn't matter.

A few yards past the girl he stopped, turned, and dropped to one knee, planting the lantern on the ground. She'd come to save him, putting her own life in danger, so there was no way he was going to leave her to fend for herself. The only reason she'd been able to pick off her targets was the light provided by his lantern. Now that he was behind her, she wouldn't be able to see as well, if at all. If they were going to get out of this mess, some teamwork was required.

"Come on, I got you!" he yelled, hoping they were operating on the same wavelength.

It seemed they were. The girl was already moving and simultaneously reaching to her quiver for yet another arrow. As she turned her back, a stone glanced off the side of her head. She yelled out in shock or pain, but the blow didn't faze her for a second.

The moment she was past him, Dylan opened fire. Six bullets slammed into the pulsating wall of flesh, knocking down bodies and forcing the ones still coming to fall over them.

His gun empty again, Dylan ran a few yards past the crouching girl, stopped, placed the lantern on the ground and rammed his last six cartridges into the still-smoking chamber as quickly as he could.

Timing the action to perfection, the girl fired an arrow, took up a new position ahead of him, and fired again. They exchanged a glance, and something unspoken passed between them. They couldn't maintain this defensive effort, and would run out of ammunition sooner rather than later.

However, by the same token the creatures couldn't continue soaking up as much damage as they were. Something had to give. The situation was fast becoming a case of who wilted first.

For the first time since the initial confrontation, Dylan felt a sense of relief and even vague optimism. There might actually be a way out of this. He couldn't quite see the light at the end of the tunnel, but he knew it was there and they were heading in the right direction.

Gaps were beginning to appear in the throbbing, pulsating mass of pale bodies that had seemed so solid and unyielding before. Between them, he and the girl had killed or injured a fair number of the creatures, perhaps twenty or more, and more had probably abandoned the pursuit in favor of easier prey.

From a standing position, he fired off another mini-volley of shots over the head of the kneeling girl. As he did so, he noticed that her quiver was almost empty.

"Only three bullets left!" he yelled.

Dylan didn't want to admit, even to himself, that two of the remaining bullets were earmarked for him and the girl, should their escape bid fail. A .44 in the head was a lot more appealing than being eaten alive.

Suddenly, a creature dropped on her from somewhere above and the girl went down with a muffled shriek. Sensing blood, the others began to swarm.

Dylan pointed the Colt and pulled back the hammer, but couldn't get a clear shot.

An awful, dark voice in his head urged him to make his getaway while the creatures were distracted. But he was quick to quiet it. The girl had risked her life for him, and there was no way he was leaving her to this terrible fate.

Instead, brandishing the Colt in one hand and his Bowie in the other, he went rampaging into the writhing mass, hitting, stabbing, and slicing as he went. Using it as a club, he brought the Colt down on the face of the nearest creature, sending it crashing to the ground, and plunged the knife into the chest of another, then quickly withdrew it and lashed out again.

At such close range, there was no chance of mistakenly hitting the girl, so he shot another creature in the torso. He then thrust the gore-streaked knife back in its scabbard, grabbed the girl by the arm, and roughly yanked her to her feet.

"Run!" he screamed.

They'd lost a lot of ground, and Dylan sensed the time for fighting back was almost over. Now, their only hope of extending their existence was to forget about the fight and find a way out.

As they scrambled along the passage, he turned and fired his last two bullets to hopefully give the creatures pause. Then, with nothing else left and no back-up plan, all he could do was throw every ounce of energy into getting him and the girl out of the mine.

At that point, the only things in their favor were the girl's bow, which she had somehow managed to cling to, and the fact that their attackers probably didn't know they'd run out of ammunition.

"It's not far," the girl gasped. "Keep going!"

Dylan wasn't sure if the words were meant to encourage him or herself. The girl was a mess. Even in the semi-darkness he could see her arms and chest were covered in deep scratches, and blood oozed from the deep gash in the side of her head where she'd been hit by the rock.

Despite his own injuries, Dylan forced his body, limbs aching and organs screaming for oxygen, ever onwards through the pain barrier. At least the girl seemed to know where they were going.

It probably wasn't the time to be asking questions, but if they were going to die in this subterranean hell, there was just one thing Dylan needed to know. "What are you doing here?"

Even in the midst of such a dire situation, the girl found time to turn and give Dylan a look filled with such contempt it made his steps falter slightly. He felt as though he was about to be scolded by his mother.

"Hear gunfire," she said. "You fire gun here, will bring trouble. So I come find you."

"By yourself?"

"I sneak off."

"Sneak off?" Dylan repeated, his brain struggling to keep up. "So nobody knows you're here?"

"Yes. I come alone. I come fight. My people at war with the monsters for long time. I want revenge. None of our men would come help anyway. They think you just stupid white man."

Something in her tone suggested that even though she'd had the decency to come and rescue him, she held a similar opinion. And he couldn't blame her. He was definitely white, and on reflection, coming into the mine alone had been a stupid thing to do. He shouldn't have come here at all. Now, it looked as though he might be responsible for not only his premature demise but the death of someone else, too.

The short exchange established one thing: if nobody knew where the girl was, nobody was coming to save them.

Yet there was hope. If she heard his shots, others might hear them, too. But judging by what she'd said, most other people would be happy to leave him to die. Even if the Chumash found the girl was missing, it was unlikely they'd figure out where she was.

Out of the corner of his eye, he saw the girl do a dainty pirouette without so much as breaking stride and fire another lethal arrow. He received another boost when he caught a fleeting glimpse of a chalk mark on the passage wall. One of his chalk marks. That confirmed they were heading in the right direction at least.

And right then, disaster struck.

Dylan tripped over his own feet and crashed to the ground. Worse than that, the lantern, for so long his saving grace, slipped from his grasp and this time it didn't survive the fall. There was the sound of glass shattering, followed by a loud *whoosh* as the remaining kerosene, now spilled on the ground, ignited to create a waist-high wall of flame behind him.

He cursed and sat on his haunches shielding his face with his arm, stunned and despondent.

"What are you doing?" the girl said, as curt and impatient as ever. "Keep going."

It was almost as if she didn't even see the fire, let alone recognize the significance of it. Perhaps it was an indication of her character, the way her people had brought her up. When faced with adversity, she didn't collapse in floods of tears or pause to lick her wounds. She adapted to the situation and did whatever needed to be done.

She was both a warrior and a survivor.

Getting to his feet, the last thing Dylan saw before he turned and ran into the pitch black was a group of pale, sightless creatures frothing at the mouth in their eagerness to satisfy their hunger for flesh. They couldn't get through the flames, the fire creating a hissing, spitting, living wall. But with limited fuel, it would burn itself out sooner rather than later. They had to make the most of this unforeseen opportunity.

"How much farther?" Dylan asked.

"Not far," was the ambiguous reply.

Chastened, Dylan invested all his energy into making his legs move faster. With no lantern and an empty gun, the only weapon he had to hand was his Bowie knife, which he held out in front of him as he ran. He could only hope they didn't encounter any more creatures because future battles would have to be fought not only in the creature's domain, but on their terms. In the dark. At least by holding the knife in front of him there was a chance he would get in the first strike.

At times the darkness seemed to be closing in around him, pressing down and suffocating him. It was all Dylan could do to keep the panic at bay. He tried to put everything else out of his mind and focus only on putting one foot in front of the other.

Moments later, with the wall of fire far behind them and now surely exhausted, Dylan saw something shimmering in the distance ahead. It looked like a tiny crack in a curtain. At first, he thought he was hallucinating, or experiencing the concussive effects of one of the bumps and bangs he'd suffered. But then, the truth dawned on him.

Sunlight.

"There!" the girl yelled.

As if on some signal, the two wounded survivors linked arms, yanking and pulling each other along as they propelled themselves toward the light.

They were going to make it.

But Dylan knew they couldn't rest. Not yet. They had to keep pushing. There would be nothing worse than coming this far and failing.

He risked a glance behind them to see if the creatures were catching up, but the tentative tendrils of light didn't penetrate the darkness and he couldn't see anything.

Now feet away, the opening of the mine was becoming a yawning chasm, resplendent with bright golden sunshine. Beyond the threshold Dylan could see rolling mountains and a blue sky. It looked like heaven, or at least salvation. As the battered and bloodied duo burst out of the shaft, relief washed over him like a cool wave.

"Get on your horse, ride away, and never come back," the girl said without slowing down as they emerged from the mine.

"Screw that," Dylan growled. "I have a better idea."

He made for the storage shack and threw open the door. Everything was as he'd left it, including the dynamite. The veins in his neck and arms bulged as he strained to pick up one of the crates and hobbled back over to the mine entrance, praying he would have enough time to do what needed to be done before the creatures came spilling out.

"What the shit you doing?" the girl yelled as she leaped on her horse. Evidently, she hadn't quite mastered swearing yet.

Dylan heard her, but didn't reply. She would see what the shit he was doing soon enough.

Turning the crate upside down, he emptied the contents just inside the mine's entrance. He couldn't resist a furtive glance inside and was relieved to see that nothing stirred in the inky blackness. But he could sense the creatures were there, just out of sight, perhaps planning another assault but reluctant to venture into the light.

They belonged to the darkness.

With the dynamite scattered on the ground, Dylan quickly reached down, picked up several sticks, and lashed them together with a length of rope he'd found discarded in the storage shack.

He wanted to create as much devastation as possible and minimize the chance of any of those creatures getting out, as well as anyone else getting in.

Dylan fumbled in his pocket for his matches, then paused. He couldn't make out anything in the darkness, but he knew those things were there and his senses were reeling. Suddenly, something propelled itself from the mouth of the mine and hit him in the chest, knocking him to the ground. The matches went flying from his hand.

It was one of the creatures, snarling and snapping at his throat. The girl was already a hundred feet down the road, and she had no arrows left. No doubt she would find some other way of dispatching the creature, but by the time she got back Dylan would be history. It would be just his luck, or lack of it, to come this far only to fall at the last hurdle.

This was one problem he was going to have to solve by himself.

Holding the squirming creature at arm's length, he manipulated his body and raised his knee just far enough to allow him to pull the Derringer out of his boot. He pushed the muzzle into the creature's sternum and let it have both barrels, then shoved the tiny corpse off and felt around in the dirt for the matches. He had to be quick. In his mind's eye he saw a seething mass of creatures lunging toward the opening...

There was just one match left. One chance. The flame spluttered as it was buffeted by the wind, but he managed to light the fuse before it died. When the flame caught, he casually lobbed the bundle on top of the other sticks at the mouth of the mine, scrambled to his feet, and jogged over to Skydance. The horse was stamping his feet and his nostrils were flaring as he strained against his rope. Dylan took a second to give his sidekick a soothing pat on the head, then untied and mounted him. The horse appeared to be almost as happy to be leaving this place as he was.

Just as he and Skydance caught up with the girl, there was a cacophonous *boom* as the dynamite blew behind them, bringing the entire side of the mountain down on the entrance to Silent Mine and showering Dylan, the girl, and their horses with dust and debris. Sealing the entrance wouldn't solve the problem of what lay inside, but it would stop anyone else going inside and disappearing. For a while, at least.

"Good job," the girl said, nodding with approval. For the first time in their short relationship, she actually looked impressed.

"Thanks. That was satisfying," Dylan replied, passing her a handful of beans he retrieved from a saddlebag.

The girl looked at him in amazement. "You crazy? How can you eat?"

"I always get hungry after I kick some ass," Dylan explained. "And we just kicked a whole lot of ass."

"Kick ass?"

"Win a fight."

"Oh. That, we did."

"Damn right."

"What now?"

"Now I'm going to ride into Hope's Creek and get the biggest steak I can find. You're welcome to join me."

"No thanks."

Half a mile later, they came to a fork in the road. Dylan nudged Skydance toward the left-hand path, while the girl steered her horse to the right. No doubt she had her own life to be getting back to, a life different from Dylan's but probably every bit as complicated and one that would forever be colored by this shared experience.

"By the way," she said, almost as an afterthought, catching his eye as she veered off. "It's Nina."

"What is?"

"My name."

-EPILOGUE-

As Dylan rode on toward town, he let his mind wander. Under normal circumstances, he might worry about the townsfolk not believing his outlandish story. To an outsider, it would sound more like a fairytale than fact. But he suspected that wouldn't be the case in Hope's Creek.

However, instead of going up there and doing anything about it, the townspeople would probably just try to sweep the whole nasty business under the carpet. As dangerous as Silent Mine was, and might still be, its lure was enough to bring people to town and God knows, the town needed that if it was going to survive.

In fairness, all the townspeople he'd talked to had made a point of telling him not to come. Same as they probably told everyone else who asked. There wasn't much else they could do to maintain their integrity. If they warned people against going up there and they went anyway, that was on them. The only thing to blame for what had happened up there was his own pig headedness. But perhaps they knew that sometimes, if you told someone not to do something, it only made them want to do it more. This insatiable thirst for freedom Americans were afflicted with wasn't always a good thing.

Besides, he got the impression that these monsters with no eyes weren't unique to Silent Mine. If the stories from Wales and elsewhere in the world were to be believed, the creatures were everywhere, like termites, and always had been. Fighting them would be like fighting the wind. The world would keep turning as it always had, mankind as oblivious to the things living beneath the surface of the earth as they were to the creatures living beneath the surface of the ocean. Dylan couldn't be responsible for what other people thought or did. But there were things he *could* affect, and ways he could make a difference.

Reaching into his pocket, he retrieved one of the thumbnail-sized gold nuggets he'd found on the nameless dead miner inside the mine, and held it up to the light. He didn't know a great deal about gold, but he imagined the nugget must be worth a tidy sum. Maybe as much as a couple of hundred bucks. Thomas Winstanley's wife would appreciate the help. It wouldn't soften the blow of losing her husband, but at least she wouldn't have to pay for a funeral. Dylan had already decided to forfeit the rest of the money she owed him. Even though he had a pretty good idea what happened to Thomas, he didn't have any proof.

He'd been thinking about what to tell the widow, even toying with the idea of making up some elaborate yet plausible story about Thomas running away and setting up with a dancing girl.

Which would be easier for her to handle? Thinking her husband was out there living it up with someone else, or thinking he was lying in an underground chamber being eaten by something straight out of a nightmare?

He decided neither option, nor anything else he could think up, was any better than another, and resolved to tell the woman everything that had happened since they'd last talked. She deserved to know the truth, then she could draw her own conclusions. When he reached Hope's Creek he would write her a long letter explaining everything and send it from the post office, along with one of the nuggets.

Then he planned to cash in the other nugget and go for that big juicy steak he'd promised himself. He might even stop by the saloon for a sour toe or two.

He could do with the extra kick.

C.M. SAUNDERS

Chris Saunders (he/him), who writes fiction as C.M. Saunders, is a writer and editor from South Wales. He has worked extensively in the publishing industry, holding desk jobs ranging from staff writer to associate editor, and is currently employed at a trade magazine. His fiction has appeared in numerous magazines, ezines and anthologies worldwide including The Literary Hatchet, Crimson Streets, 34 Orchard, Phantasomagoria, and DOA volumes I and III, while his books have been both traditionally and independently published. He has several novellas and six volumes of short fiction available, while his latest release is *The Wretched Bones: A Ben Shivers Mystery*, on Midnight Machinations, an imprint of Grinning Skull Press.

Bibliography

Also by C.M. Saunders

Full-length Non-Fiction Books:

Into the Dragon's Lair – A Supernatural History of
Wales (2003, Gwasg Carreg Gwalch)
From the Ashes – The REAL Story of Cardiff City FC
(2013, Gwasg Carreg Gwalch)

Novels:

Rainbow's End (2012, FlareFont Publishing) (OUT
OF PRINT)
Sker House (2016, DeadPixel Publications)
The Wretched Bones: A Ben Shivers Mystery (2023,
Midnight Machinations)

Novellas:

Apartment 14F: An Oriental Ghost story (2009, Damnation Books)

Dead of Night (2010 Damnation Books)

Devil's Island (2012, Rainstorm Press)

Out of Time (2014, DeadPixels Publications)

No Man's Land: Horror in the Trenches (2016, Deviant Dolls Publications)

Apartment 14F: An Oriental Ghost Story (Uncut) (2017, Deviant Dolls Publications)

Human Waste (2017, Deviant Dolls Publications)

Dead of Night (Uncut) (2018, Deviant Dolls Publications)

Tethered (2020, Terror Tract Publishing)

Silent Mine: A Dylan Decker Mystery (2024, Undertaker Books)

Collections:

X: A Collection of Horror (2014, DeadPixel Publications)

X2: Another Collection of Horror (2015, DeadPixel Publications)

X Sample (2017, Deviant Dolls Publications)

X3 (2018, Deviant Dolls Publications)

X: Omnibus (2019, Deviant Dolls Publications)

X4 (2020, Deviant Dolls Publications)

Back from the Dead: A Collection of Zombie Fiction
(2021)

X5 (2022)

X6 (2024)

Undertaker Books

www.undertakerbooks.com

If you are a fan of horror stories and tales,
you'll want to follow Undertaker Books.

We're bringing you stories to take to your grave.

SIGN UP FOR OUR NEWSLETTER ONLINE

Printed in Great Britain
by Amazon

56251350R00086